LOST AND FOUND

A CHARLIE MACCREADY MYSTERY

James M. McCracken

CONTENTS

DEDICATION

In memory of my high school best friend,
Howard Franklin Miller.
1959 – 2001
Never forgotten.
Always in my heart.

ACKNOWLEDGMENTS

With heartfelt appreciation to Dennis Blakesley, Barbara Blair, Melissa Ainsworth, Michael Anne Maslow, Anthony & Pushpa Huff, Betsy Jones, and Phyllis Liesegang for their constant encouragement.

A TROUBLING OF GOLDFISH

Charlie MacCready sat on the cement bench beneath a dogwood tree on the Great Lawn in front of Saint Michael's Abbey and watched the goldfish in the pond at his feet. They darted around in the deep water as though playing tag with each other, without a care in the world. Charlie wished his life were as simple as theirs. He looked up at the clear blue August sky. There was a faint wisp of white where a cloud was beginning to form.

"You did it again," said the middle-aged priest sitting beside him.

Charlie looked at Father Cecil. "Did what?" A lock of his auburn hair fell across his eyebrows. He swiped it away and made a mental note to see Brother Simon about a haircut.

"Sighed," Father Cecil answered. His dark sunglasses hid his sightless eyes from view. "What's the matter?"

"Nothing," Charlie said. Deep down inside, he wished he could confide in his friend, but he had promised his grandmother and his great-uncle he would not talk about it to anyone.

"Oh, I see," Father Cecil said, and nodded. "I may be blind, son, but as you know, I can hear very well. Just as I heard a goldfish break the surface of the water just now."

Charlie looked down at the pond and saw a tiny ripple. "You heard that?" he asked in amazement.

"Yes. Do you know what a group of goldfish are called?" he asked.

"A school?"

Father Cecil nodded his head slightly. "Some may call them that, but that term is used more for fish in the ocean. The poetic term is a troubling."

"That doesn't fit these goldfish," Charlie said, looking back at the pond.

"Why is that?"

"They have such carefree lives, swimming around, playing all day. They don't seem to be troubled by anything. I wish I were a goldfish."

"You do? Really?"

"Yeah, then I wouldn't have to worry about anything," Charlie answered.

"Trust me, son, their lives are anything but trouble-free. Did you know that people who sell goldfish sometimes refer to them as feeder fish?"

"Feeder fish?" Charlie's eyebrows pinched above his nose and he looked at the priest beside him. "Why's that?"

"Because people with big aquariums use goldfish as food for their larger fish."

"They do?" Charlie said, his voice raising an octave. He looked down at the goldfish in the pond and then back at Father Cecil. "That's horrible."

"It's part of life. No one and no thing lives a trouble-free life. Everyone has something that worries them. Maybe a goldfish doesn't feel things the same way we do because they aren't aware that they are alive, but they still feel. God has lovingly given them something called instinct. Intuitively they know how to spot and avoid danger."

"Wow," Charlie sighed and looked at the goldfish again. "I never thought that much about them. I just figured they were, well, fish."

"The point is, son, we all have troubles. We humans were not implanted with the same instinct God gave the animals. God wanted us to be like him. So, he gave us self-awareness, a sense of being. But along with it comes the knowledge that we are mortal and fragile. So, for the times when our troubles seem too much of a burden to carry, he gave us each other to lean on."

"I get it," Charlie said, realizing where Father Cecil was headed with his analogy. "I can't talk about it. I promised Father Abbot and my grandma I wouldn't."

"I see," Father Cecil nodded again. "So, your mood has to do with your family, your dad's father and the letter?"

Charlie's eyes widened and he looked both shocked and surprised. "You know about that?"

Father Cecil nodded. "Yes, son. Over the past four months, I noticed a change in you. You seem quieter, troubled. When you wouldn't talk about what was bothering you, I went to Abbot Ambrose. He told me about your grandfather and the letter."

"I'm just so confused," Charlie said, his shoulders sagged as if a weight had been removed. "It feels like everything I believed was a lie. I mean, am I Charlie MacCready or Charlie O'Sullivan?"

"Who do you think you are?"

"I don't know anymore. I feel so empty inside. Like I vanished."

"Son, I wouldn't put too much importance on a name. Names can change. But that doesn't change who you are inside. Take Mister Duggan for example. Before he joined the monastery, he was known as Dougary, a name that struck fear in others because he was a hoodlum. But once he finishes his postulancy, he will be known by the name Jonah, which means peace."

Charlie nodded but did not speak.

"Charlie, let me try to explain it another way. Take a painting for example. Up close, you see all the imperfections left by the paintbrush. The way one of the hairs on the brush broke loose from the others and made a small line of its own on the canvas. If we focus too much on the flaw, we will never see the beauty of the bigger picture.

"Charlie, you are a good, loving, and caring young man. Regardless of the name your grandfather made for himself and even the one your father made for him, you are you. You will make your own name. Do you understand?"

Again, Charlie nodded.

"Son, I can't hear you head rattle, you need to use your words," Father Cecil said, and playfully bumped shoulders with Charlie.

"It makes sense," Charlie answered, but still he could not shake how lost he felt.

"So, tell me, how was your summer helping out in the fields?"

"If I ever see another strawberry, green bean, or cucumber again, I'll puke." Charlie said, looking at his cracked and stained hands.

Father Cecil smiled to himself. "I know how you feel. Before I lost my sight, I used to help the brothers in the fields too. It's a backbreaking job. So, does this mean you are looking forward to school starting up?"

"I guess," Charlie answered, slipping back into depression.

"Are you worried about something?"

"Father, do you think my parents are okay? I mean, my grandmother said they went into hiding because someone threatened to expose my dad. Do you think the mob caught up with them, and that's why they never came for me?"

"I seriously doubt the Irish Mafia ever made it this far west, at least, if they have, I've never heard of it. But, then again, I don't suppose they would go around advertising it if they were here, would they? I honestly don't know."

"I wish I knew what happened to them."

"I know, son. But, someday it will all be made clear."

"Yeah, that's what everyone keeps telling me." Charlie let

out another sigh.

"You're doing it again," Father Cecil said, giving Charlie's knee a pat. "Is there something else?"

"I don't know. I just have a lot on my mind."

"I imagine you do. You're standing at the cusp of beginning your own life as an adult. You have your future ahead of you. It's now time to decide what you want to do with your life."

"Yeah. Something like that."

"Still, you're bothered by the letter, your parents, and your name. Son, try to think of it this way, your grandparents did what they thought was best for their son, your father. They sent him to us so he would have a better chance at a good life. Your parents gave you to your grandmother because they wanted you to have a life of your own and not one where you would have to constantly look over your shoulder or live in fear. They wouldn't want you to spend your life stuck in the past."

"It's not—oh, forget it," Charlie said, sounding discouraged.

"Son, I hope by now you would know that you can tell me anything and it will remain between us."

"I know," Charlie answered.

"Then, tell me, what is it?" Father Cecil said, turning toward Charlie.

"I just feel confused inside. I know my parents wanted the best for me when they left me with my grandmother, but, at the same time, I'm angry with them for leaving me behind and not coming back for me like they promised. And now, everything I had hoped for, for nearly fifteen years, will never happen. We're *never* going to be a family. Rick was right."

"Master Walters?"

"Yes. He said my parents would never come for me and that I was wasting my time hoping they would. Now, I'm not even sure I would want them in my life if they did come back."

"That's a bit harsh, don't you think?"

"But it's how I feel."

Father Cecil nodded. "I understand, but, son, don't let it eat at you. You need to let go of your disappointment and anger."

"Why should I? They are the ones who lied."

"Oh, Charlie," Father Cecil said, and frowned. "I once heard a talk where someone likened holding onto resentment to drinking a glass of poison and hoping the other person died. Son, your anger will only rob you of living. You will be stuck in the past and miss out on possibly a wonderful future."

Charlie did not respond. He looked back at the goldfish swimming in the pond and let his friend's words sink in. "I'll try," he said.

"That's all I ask. What time is it?"

Charlie pulled his pocket watch out and opened it. "It's nearly an hour before for Vespers."

"Well, we should be getting back to the abbey."

The two stood up and carefully moved away from the edge of the pond. As they headed back to the four-story brick building, Father Cecil rested his hand on Charlie's shoulder. With every step he felt Charlie's shoulder tense up a bit more.

"So, have you heard from Master Miller?"

"No," Charlie answered. "I don't think Howard wants to be my friend anymore."

"What?" Father Cecil said, sounding shocked. "Why would you think that?"

"I haven't heard from him all summer. He stopped answering my letters, and there's no answer whenever I call him. What am I supposed to think?"

Father Cecil's lips curled into a sympathetic smile. "Not that, I'm sure. Charlie, a lot of young men your age who are out there in the world get a summer job. Perhaps that's all this is?"

"You think?" Charlie asked, surprised that the thought never occurred to him.

"Yes, I do. Don't give up on him or your friendship. Keep writing him. I'm sure he loves hearing from you even if he doesn't write back."

"Okay."

Father Cecil smiled as he sensed Charlie's dark mood lifting. The two continued to walk across the Great Lawn.

Once they reached the Abbey and entered the monastery wing, the two walked in silence. However, try as he might to think about something else, thoughts of his parents kept resurfacing in Charlie's mind and with it a feeling of resentment mixed with a bit of worry. He tried to focus on something else but the stark hallway, devoid of any décor, gave him little inspiration. He stopped when he reached the door to Father Cecil's cell.

"Here we are," Charlie said quietly. He still thought it was strange that the monks called their rooms a cell. It sounded as if they were in a prison, but Father Cecil had explained the word cell came from the Latin word for room. Still, seeing the furnishings inside the small room, Charlie could not shake the prison image.

"Thank you, son," Father Cecil said. He paused, hand on the doorknob. "Please think about what I said. You have your whole future ahead of you. I'm sure your parents wouldn't want you to stop living because of worrying about them for the rest of your life."

"I know, and I will," Charlie sighed. "I'll see you later."

"Good. I look forward to it."

Charlie took the long route back to his dorm. Instead of cutting across the balcony on the second floor of the main foyer, he took the stairs down to the first floor and passed by the monastery's reception desk and into the foyer. The daylight reflected off the polished white marble tiles on the floor. Above, the brass and crystal chandelier sparkled. Charlie had become used to the opulence and barely noticed it anymore.

He pulled the door to the student wing open and entered the hallway. The off-white walls and concrete floor were a sharp contrast to the foyer's decor, another thing that Charlie paid little attention to. He headed past Abbot Ambrose's office on his right and Father Mark's office to his left. His eyes were focused on the wall outside the refectory where the students' mail slots were. Even from down the hall he could see his mail slot was empty. When he reached the stairs, he headed up to the fourth floor.

For the past four years, Saint Nicholas dorm had been his home. The dormitory had eight cubicles, four on either side of the large room, with at least one bed and nightstand in each, some had bunkbeds. In the center of the room was a lounge area. A braided oval rug of browns, golds, and greens lay on the floor in the exact center. A dark green and gold plaid overstuffed sofa sat facing two matching chairs. An old antique steamer trunk, topped with a thick sheet of glass, sat between the sofa and chairs and served as a coffee table, but the boys used it as a footrest more than anything else. Charlie stared at it as he walked past. Learning that it had belonged to his father and that it had held the answer to the mysterious key he wore around his neck for the past four years was still a bit overwhelming.

The dorm was quiet. The regular seminarians had gone home to their families at the beginning of summer. The only other resident boy in Saint Nicholas, Ted Wilson, had been reassigned to Saint Thomas dorm, leaving Charlie alone. Charlie stopped when he reached his cubicle in the far left corner. Before going home, his fellow classmate and bunkmate, Rick Walters, was moved to Saint Peter dorm to be its prefect when school resumed in September. That meant Charlie had the six-foot by eight-foot cubicle all to himself.

The first thing Charlie did after Rick moved out was move his bed back to the corner beneath the window that overlooked the Great Lawn. He placed his nightstand beside the head of his bed and put an overstuffed chair—that he had claimed from a former senior's cubicle—in the corner between the nightstand and the partition that separated his cubicle from the Muster twins' cubicle. Lastly, he put the desk and chair Dougary had given him against the partition across from the foot of his bed.

Removing his black blazer, Charlie draped it over the back of his desk chair. He stopped and looked at the framed picture of his parents that sat on his desk. Where he once saw love, their smiling faces now seemed to taunt Charlie, reminding him that what he hoped for was not going to happen. He turned the picture face down on his desk and clasped the locket around his neck, the one that held the tiny photographs of his parents. For now, out of sight beneath his shirt, it would stay where it was. He pulled out his chair and sat down. He opened the desk drawer, took out a piece of stationary, and began writing a letter to his grandmother.

Dear Grandma,

I hope you are doing well. Please excuse my handwriting. My hands, arms, back, everything is still sore from working in the fields with the brothers all summer. I had no idea they grew their own fruits and vegetables. I'll be glad when school starts in two weeks so I can rest.

You remember my friend, Father Cecil? Well, he says I need to start thinking about what I want to do with my life. But, Grandma, I don't know what I want to be. I mean, I always thought my parents would have returned for me before now. We were supposed to be a family. Father Cecil says I'm no longer a child. I know that, but part of me can't move on until I know what happened to my parents. You understand, don't you? Do you know where they are?

Grandma, I know I promised not to tell anyone about the letter and the box, but can't I tell Howard? He's my best friend. I trust him. Besides, he was helping me figure out the mystery of the key, the medal, and the watch. He deserves to know that it's solved. I know he won't tell anyone. Please.

Charlie signed his name with his usual closing words then stuffed the letter into an envelope. He addressed it, and put a stamp on it. Glancing at the clock above the entry doors, he saw it was time for Vespers, and then dinner afterward. His stomach growled at the thought.

Charlie put his pen and the unused stationary back into the drawer of his desk, grabbed his coat, and headed downstairs to the Abbey Church. He would drop the letter into the outgoing mail slot on his way.

After Vespers concluded, Charlie met the other five boys outside the monastery's refectory. It had been decided at the start of summer by their dean, Father Mark, and Abbot Ambrose that the boys would join the brothers for dinner. For breakfast and lunch, they would be on their own. They would pick up their trays in the kitchen and dine in their own refectory. At first Charlie resisted the idea of eating with the monks, but now he did not mind it so much. The brothers at his table were interesting and nice.

Charlie especially liked talking with Brother Linus. He always had interesting stories to share, much to the dismay of Brother Humilitas. Brother Linus had been an actor on Broadway and even played a role in the musical *Hair* and *Cabaret* before joining the abbey. When Charlie asked Brother Linus if he were going to act in a play since there was a beautiful stage in the new gymnasium, Brother Humilitas's eyes went wide and his jaw tightened.

"Absolutely not!" he answered for Brother Linus.

Brother Linus looked shocked at first but then softened his expression and gave Charlie a wink. "It is up to Abbot Ambrose. If he were to ask, I would obey. I shall not presume to suggest or even broach the subject with him."

While Charlie stood in line behind Ted Wilson outside the refectory, he glanced over his shoulder and saw Father Vicar approaching. The tall, gaunt monk, whose expression was more sinister than holy, straightened his back and stretched his neck until he looked down his beaky nose at them. Without a word, he entered the refectory.

"I can't believe Father Abbot made him principal," Ted said without turning around.

"I guess he had his reasons," Charlie answered, but inside, he felt the same way as Ted. Of all the monks, why Father Vicar?

Once Father Mark arrived, the boys followed him into the

refectory and dispersed to their assigned tables.

Dinner was silent. Three postulants took turns reading from the Bible as everyone else ate their meal. When the second postulant took over the reading, Charlie recognized the voice immediately, but he did not dare to turn around to see if he was right. Instead, he listened while Dougary read.

After the meal concluded, Abbot Ambrose clapped a small block of wood against the table to get everybody's attention. Charlie looked at his great-uncle. For a brief moment, their eyes met and the corners of the Abbot's lips curled upward ever so slightly before he bowed his head. Charlie did the same while the closing prayer was said.

The next morning, Charlie rose early. As sacristan, part of his duty was to fill in for the abbey's sacristan if necessary, and since the abbey's sacristan was away on a retreat, Charlie's services were needed. Alone in the sacristy of the Abbey Church, Charlie checked the list on the small bulletin board to see which priest was officiating. He would begin by preparing the priest's chalice. He went to the vault to retrieve Father Mark's chalice. He unlocked the door with the key entrusted to him by the abbey's sacristan. He unlocked the heavy thick steel door and pulled it open. Inside the vault was a large room. The three outer walls were covered floor to ceiling with large square cubbyholes. Each cubby held one chalice, some encrusted with jewels, others plain gold, some silver, and even one made of pottery. In one of the cubbies, Charlie noticed his father's metal box. Pushing his anxiety down, he quickly located Father Mark's chalice and locked the vault door as he left.

Back in the sacristy, Charlie set the chalice on the counter. He carefully draped the purification cloth across its top, making sure the embossed cross in the center faced down into the chalice. Next, he placed the paten with a large host on top of the cloth. He picked up the white square pall and placed it on top of the paten. Finally, he took the chalice veil from the vestment drawer and carefully draped it over the chalice. When he was finished, he stood back and examined the covered chalice. Something did not look right. It was missing something. He opened the vestment drawer and found the matching burse, the square folder that held the cloth the priest would use to set the chalice upon on the altar. He took it and placed it on top, making sure the decorative cloth side was face up. Satisfied that he had not forgotten anything else, he began laying out the vestments.

Being the sacristan was a lot more work than Charlie had imagined. There were so many details and rituals involved. The previous sacristans had made it look so easy. Still, Charlie felt honored being named this year's sacristan.

Thirty minutes prior to the start of Mass, Father Ignatius entered the sacristy.

"Good morning, Master MacCready," he greeted Charlie with a toothy grin.

"Good morning," Charlie answered, sounding a bit confused. He glanced at the schedule again. Father Mark was scheduled for the Mass.

Father Ignatius walked over to the vestments and frowned. "Father Mark couldn't make it today," he said. "So, I'm filling in."

"Oh," Charlie gasped. Father Ignatius was a whole head shorter than Father Mark. The alb Charlie had laid out would be too long for him. He quickly retrieved a shorter alb.

"Father, may I ask you a question?" Charlie asked while he laid out the alb.

"Certainly."

"Since you're the abbey's historian, I was wondering if you could tell me how a person would go about finding someone?"

Father Ignatius furrowed his brow, looking puzzled and curious at the same time. He scratched his nearly bald head. "That's a tough assignment. I suppose he could check census records? Exactly whom are you trying to find?"

"My parents," Charlie answered.

"Ah, that's a completely different story. It's near impossible to find someone who doesn't want to be found, Master MacCready."

"Isn't there some way?" Charlie asked, sounding defeated.

"I'm sorry," Father Ignatius said with a frown. "If it were just anyone, a person could check newspapers and telephone books, things like that, but someone who is hiding wouldn't use their real name."

"I guess that makes sense. Thank you, Father. Everything's ready now," he said and stepped away from the vestments. "I'll get your chalice," Charlie said, picking up Father Mark's chalice and heading back to the vault.

THE STUDENTS RETURN

Charlie found it hard to sleep, but sleep finally came. When the morning bell rang out, he awoke with the same feeling of excited anticipation as if it were Christmas. Today, the other boys were returning to the abbey to begin the school year. Finally, life would return to normal. Instead of summer being fun and exciting, it had felt like torture, with days of working in the hot sun, sweating and dirty, covered in berry juice, and afterward, boredom and too much time to think. Charlie quickly showered and dressed. When the bell rang for breakfast, he hurried downstairs to the refectory.

Instead of grabbing a tray from the kitchen, the boys entered and took their place at the table in front of the head table. After saying grace, Father Mark asked Ted Wilson to be the server for the meal.

Charlie ate his breakfast quickly, as if by eating faster it would cause time to pick up its pace. He finished his meal and sat sipping a cup of coffee while he waited for the others to catch up.

With the tables cleared, Ted took his seat again. Father Mark stood behind the head table and leaned on the back of his chair.

"The boys should begin arriving in an hour," he said with a smile and glint in his blue eyes. He adjusted his gold-rimmed glasses before he continued. "I would like all of you to be waiting out front with me to help welcome the new students and assist them in finding their dorms and cubicles. Yes, Master Wilson," he said, upon seeing Ted's hand raise.

"Do you want us to stay with them, the new guys, I mean?"

"No, just stay long enough for them to begin unpacking. We will have twenty new students this year along with our returning students. So, I will need your help. Be quick but don't make them feel rushed."

Everyone nodded in agreement.

"Very well," he said and picked up a thin stack of papers and handed each of the boys a sheet. "This is a list of the students and their dorm assignments. Brother Simon will post on each door to the dorm a chart showing the cubicle assignments. Are there any questions?"

Charlie quickly scanned the list. Rick Walters was still assigned to Saint Peter and there was an asterisk after his name to indicate he would be the prefect. Ted Wilson's name was listed with Saint Thomas. Charlie was still in Saint Nicholas dorm and to his surprise, he would be its prefect.

"Master MacCready?" Father Mark said.

Charlie looked up from the list and noticed everyone was looking at him. He looked at the dean. "Yes, Father?"

Father Mark took a deep breath before answering, something Charlie had come to recognize as a sign the dean was not pleased. "I said, I have a special assignment for you and need you to stay beside me."

"Yes, Father," Charlie answered.

"Very well, let us pray."

Father Mark offered the closing grace and the boys left the refectory. Some headed upstairs but Charlie, Ted, and a couple younger boys followed Father Mark down the main hall toward the foyer.

"I wonder why he chose you for a special assignment?" Ted whispered to Charlie.

"Beats me," Charlie answered. "I didn't sign up for anything."

"You must be the dean's pet, just like you are with Abbot Ambrose." There was a hint of jealousy in Ted's tone that caused Charlie's back to stiffen.

"Why do you think that?" he asked.

"Oh, come on, everybody knows you get away with murder around here. If I did even one fraction of the stuff you did, I would have been kicked out of here a long time ago."

"That's not true," Charlie protested.

"Oh yeah, well, I've been here longer than you, and I've never seen Black Butte, much less the attic or the belfry. Ask anyone. I'm not making it up. You get special dispensation."

"No, I don't. That was more Howard Miller's doing— except for Black Butte, that was me, but I got in trouble for it."

"Oh, big woo, an hour of work crew."

Charlie's brow furrowed and he clenched his teeth when he felt his anger start to boil, then suddenly, he forced himself to relax. "I don't know what your problem is, Ted, but you're not going to get to me."

"I wasn't trying to get to you. I was just making an observation. That's all," Ted said in a condescending tone.

Charlie shook his head and let Ted walk ahead of him. He looked at the back of the tall, thin, dark haired boy and remembered when they first met. Ted had been a stocky, short kid with a round face then. In the last four years, he grew taller and thinner and was now almost an inch taller than Father Mark. Charlie, at five foot eleven, was now the shorter one.

Father Mark returned to his office, while the boys headed outside to the front steps. Ted and the other boys stopped at the top of the steps, leaned against the side railing, and spoke in hushed whispers. Charlie ignored them and proceeded down the steps. At the bottom, he turned right and headed to his favorite thinking spot.

The morning air was nippy. Charlie dug his hands deeper into the pockets of his black slacks. His blazer, unbuttoned, provided little warmth for his chest. Even the lightweight white shirt and green and gold striped necktie did little to fend off the chill. Charlie's only hope was that the sun would melt the morning clouds soon.

He walked with determination along the dirt path beside the back road. It led from the parking lot at the rear of the student wing of the Abbey, around the east side of the hill past the cemetery, candle and pottery shack, and pig barns before it connected with the main driveway to and from the abbey. Charlie did not have to think about where he was headed. After four years, his feet knew the way.

Charlie stopped when he reached the ivy-covered stone fence to the right of the path. He put his hand on the rusted, wrought iron gate and pulled the latch free. The gate swung inward with a bit of complaint. Charlie glanced over his shoulder and spotted Ted and another boy standing behind a fir tree on the Great Lawn. The small cloud that appeared above them told Charlie what they were up to. He turned back and slipped into the private courtyard. A concrete and stone bench, large enough for three or four people to rest and reflect comfortably, was built against the stone wall. Charlie sat down and leaned his back against the wall.

Across from the bench, rising above the small courtyard, a purposeful pile of rocks formed a grotto. Standing in the alcove was a life-size statue of the Virgin Mary. Charlie smiled to himself, remembering how Steven, the sacristan the year Charlie came to the abbey, had dubbed the statue Our Lady of the Subway, much to the chagrin of the Abbot and other monks. He called her that because behind her was the opening to a tunnel that led to the abbey's garages on the other side of the Great Lawn where the gymnasium now stood. The tunnel had been sealed off after a fire two years ago had destroyed the garages. Now, a sheet of plexiglass placed in front of the statue protected it from the weather, and kept curious boys from attempting to go into the tunnel.

Alone with his thoughts, Ted's words did sting a bit as they replayed in Charlie's mind. He wished he had a better comeback than just saying his accusation was not true. But deep down, he knew it was a lie. It was not that he was the Abbot's pet, he was the Abbot's great-nephew, a secret he had kept from the other boys for nearly five years, and one he was not about to share.

The creaking of the gate jolted Charlie from his musings. His first thought was he had not latched the gate properly, but then he saw Sister Faith enter the courtyard. Her black veil hung past her shoulders, creating a blinder of sorts. Her back was toward Charlie as she closed the gate. When she turned around and saw him, she let out a gasp.

"Oh! I'm sorry, Master MacCready," she said, putting her fingers to her lips. "Forgive me, I didn't know anyone was here."

"It's okay, Sister," Charlie said and stood up. He gestured for her to sit beside him.

Over the past year, Charlie had grown fond of Sister Faith. There was something about her that made him feel as if he could tell her anything. At first, he thought it was because she shared his mother's name, but he soon realized it was because of her gentleness and sincere concern.

"I come by every now and again on my break from the kitchen to make sure Our Lady's courtyard is neat and tidy. I hope I wasn't interrupting anything," she explained.

"No, I just got here myself. I come here to think," Charlie said.

"Oh, I imagine you have a lot to think about, this being your senior and final year here," she said with a smile and twinkle in her blue eyes.

Charlie felt his stomach muscles tighten as a feeling of nausea sweep over him. He swallowed and willed the feeling to pass.

"It's not just about that," he said. "Father Mark just told me he has a special assignment for me. Then, I keep wondering why

Howard hasn't answered any of my letters. He always writes back right after receiving a letter from me, but it's been months since I've heard from him. I keep writing but he hasn't written back. And then there's another matter I promised my grandma I wouldn't talk about."

"Oh, I see," Sister Faith said, nodding her head and glancing at the statue above them. "Well, I can't help you with the first issue because I don't know what it is, either. The last issue is also an unknown. But perhaps Master Miller has a summer job and is tired from working all day? A lot of boys your age get jobs in the fields or in one of those fast food restaurants."

"Maybe," Charlie said. "Or maybe he's just forgotten about me and doesn't want to be my friend anymore?"

"Oh, now stop that. You two are best friends. He hasn't forgotten you."

"But—"

"Ut-ut! Don't go down that path."

"What path?"

"Self-pity," she answered. "Feeling sorry for yourself isn't going to do anything except make you depressed."

"I suppose you're right."

"Suppose?" Sister Faith said, sounding offended. "I *am* right, Master MacCready," she added with a grin and wink.

Charlie laughed. They bumped shoulders.

"Now, when do the boys begin arriving?" she asked, changing the subject.

"I don't know. Father Mark said in an hour or so. He wants all of us to join him on the front steps to welcome the newbies."

"Well, that sounds like fun."

"I suppose. I just wish Howard would write."

"Ah, there you go again," Sister Faith said. "What do you say, once you've finished with whatever special assignment Father Mark has for you, you come to the kitchen and we'll see if we can't get in touch with Master Miller?"

"I've tried calling him. He doesn't answer."

"Well, we could give it another shot. After all, what have we to lose?"

Charlie nodded and then looked at her. She was smiling at him with the face of an angel. "Sure."

Looking at the small pendant watch that was pinned to the left breast of her habit, Sister Faith gasped. "Oh my, my break is over, I need to get back to the kitchen, lunch isn't going to fix itself." She stood up and headed for the gate. Stopping, she looked back. "Just remember, Master MacCready, come see me later."

"I will. Thank you, Sister," Charlie said. He watched her close the gate as she left. Turning back around, he looked up at the statue of Our Lady of the Subway.

The sound of someone running along the path caused Charlie to stand up. Ted stopped when he reached the grotto gate. He held onto it and tried to catch his breath.

"What's up?" Charlie asked.

"Father Mark," he said between breaths, "wants to see you under the portico right away."

"Okay," Charlie said. As he slipped through the gate, he got a whiff of Ted. "You really should lay off the cigarettes," he whispered.

"What?" Ted asked, with feigned ignorance.

"You heard me," Charlie said with a grin. "See ya."

Charlie hurried back to the Abbey. As he approached the main entrance, he heard the sound of a car approaching.

"If this is who I think it is, you made it back just in time," Father Mark said.

"Sorry, Father, I was talking to Sister Faith."

"No worries, son," Father Mark said while he continued to watch a brown sedan make its way slowly up the drive on the west edge of Great Lawn.

"Who is it?" Charlie asked.

"You'll see," Father Mark answered with a grin.

The car pulled to a stop at the foot of the steps beneath the portico. Charlie started to take a step toward the car but

Father Mark's firm hand on his arm, stopped him.

"Wait here," he said.

Charlie faced the dean and gave him a confused look. "What's the—"

"Hi, Charlie!" a familiar voice called out.

Charlie looked at the car at the bottom of the steps. He immediately recognized the dark curly haired driver with black rimmed glasses. It was Howard. He was a bit taller and thinner since Charlie had seen him last, but it was him.

Mr. Miller climbed out of the passenger side, closing the door behind him. He walked toward the trunk.

"Howard!" Charlie yelled. Father Mark released his hold and let Charlie rush down the steps to greet his friend. The two hugged in front of the car. "I'm so happy to see you," he said.

"Me too," Howard said as they parted. "I got your letters."

"Yeah! Why didn't you write back?" Charlie said, playfully slugging Howard on the shoulder.

"Sorry. It was a crazy summer."

"Well, you picked a great day for a visit. The students are returning today."

"I know."

Glancing up the stairs at the dean, Charlie said. "Father Mark has me greeting the newbies. I'll ask if we can visit. When do you have to leave?"

"Next summer," Howard said.

"Wha—" Just then Mr. Miller set Howard's suitcases down on the sidewalk. Charlie looked at them and then back at Howard.

"I think that's all of it," Mr. Miller said.

"What? Are you staying?" Charlie asked.

"Yes. Dad said it was only right for me to graduate with my friends. So, I'm here for the year."

Again, Charlie threw his arms around Howard and gave him a hug. "This is great," he said and turned to Mr. Miller.

"Thank you, sir."

Mr. Miller gave a short laugh. "No problem." He stepped toward Howard. "Well, son, see you in a month. Maybe you could even bring Charlie home with you for the weekend?"

"Sure," Howard said. "Thanks for letting me drive."

"You need the practice," Mr. Miller said, and took back the keys from his son. "Take good care of them, Father," he called to Father Mark.

"We shall," he answered back. He descended the steps and held out his hand to Howard. "Welcome back, Master Miller," he greeted with a handshake. "Let's see, you are in Saint Thomas dorm."

"Saint Thomas?" Charlie objected.

"Yes, Saint Thomas," Father Mark repeated. "You will be the prefect this year. I trust you know your duties."

"Yes, Father."

"But why can't he be in Saint Nicholas again?" Charlie objected.

"He is needed elsewhere, Master MacCready. We all go to where we are assigned."

"But—"

"Hey, it's okay, Charlie," Howard said. "We will still have plenty of time together."

"I suppose so."

"Why don't you help Master Miller with his suitcases and then the two of you can come back down and help me greet the rest of the new students," Father Mark suggested, though his tone left them no options.

"Sure, Father," Charlie said as he started up the front steps toward the entrance. "Come on, let's go find your cubicle."

"Don't dawdle. Be quick," Father Mark said as they entered the abbey building.

"We won't—I mean, we will," Charlie said, unsure of which was the correct response. He held the door open for Howard and then followed him into the abbey.

"Well, this all looks familiar," Howard said with a hint of sarcasm.

"Yeah, they're not much for color here," Charlie agreed with a laugh as he looked at the off-white walls and grey, polished concrete floor of the main hallway of the student wing. "I can't believe you're actually here."

Howard laughed. "Well, I am."

The two found Howard's new cubicle in Saint Thomas dorm. It was in the corner with two windows. The one looked to the east and gave a view of the forest, the other to the south and Black Butte.

"Not exactly the same view as you had in Saint Nicholas," Charlie said.

"No, but at least the sun won't wake me up," Howard laughed.

After putting the two suitcases down on the bed, the boys returned to the main entrance.

THE NEW HANGOUT

The next day, while the new students had an orientation meeting in the main lounge on the fourth floor, Charlie and Howard took a walk outside. The air was warm, and felt thick. Howard left his blazer in his dorm. He tugged at the collar of his white shirt while he led the way.

"I don't know why we have to wear this stupid noose," he groused, and loosened his necktie. "I prefer our old uniforms. At least the air could circulate better."

"Yeah, I miss them, too," Charlie agreed. "So, where are we going?"

"Since the belfry is locked. I thought I'd show you our new hangout."

Charlie grew concerned when they reached the chain that stretched across the entrance to the road that led to Black Butte. He watched Howard step over the chain.

"Hey, we're not allowed."

"Don't be such a wuss."

"A what?"

"A wuss. A baby."

"Oh, so now you're calling me names?"

Howard laughed. "I was only teasing."

"Well, I don't like that word, and I'm not a baby."

"Okay, I'm sorry, just come on. Have I ever led you astray?"

"Do you really want me to answer that?"

The two laughed. Eventually, Charlie stepped across the chain after making sure no one was around or watching.

"We're not allowed to be on Black Butte."

"I know."

"The ground isn't stable. Remember?"

"I remember. We're not going there."

Charlie looked around as they continued to walk along the road that led to site of the old burned down abbey. "Then why are we going this way?"

"You'll see. Relax. I have it all under control," Howard said.

Once they were almost to the top of Black Butte and with the ruins in view, Howard left the road and headed east, down the hill and into what Charlie thought looked like an old orchard. The trees, some dead, were all evenly spaced. Their trunks were gnarled and their branches were creepy-looking, even with leaves.

"What is this place?" he asked.

"It's what's left of the apple orchard. The brothers abandoned it after the fire destroyed the old abbey. They said the smoke and all had damaged the trees and the apples weren't any good after that."

"Is that true?"

"I don't know," Howard said. "Anyway, they planted a new orchard on their property in the valley."

"I know it all too well," Charlie said, looking at his hands and remembering how he spent several days picking apples at the end of summer break. "Why didn't they cut this orchard down?"

"Don't know that either. I wasn't around back then," Howard said with a laugh. "In any case, here we are." Howard stopped and held his arms out wide. "Ta-da! Our new hangout."

Charlie looked at the small cabin. It reminded him of the Tin Man's house in the movie *The Wizard of Oz* that they watched every year at Easter. The roof was covered in thick green moss. The outside walls were unpainted boards. The windows were still unbroken, much to Charlie's surprise and bewilderment. "Where did you hear about this?"

"Oh, I've known about it for a long time," Howard answered, as if it were no big deal. "I overheard some of the older guys talking about it when I was new here. So, one day, I followed one of them out here."

"I thought you told me you never came out to Black Butte."

"Technically, it was the truth. I never went as far as the ruins."

"Technically," Charlie repeated, and pursed his lips.

"Come on, let's go inside."

"Wait," Charlie said, grabbing Howard's arm and stopping him while he eyed the small house. "It's not going to fall down on us, is it?"

Howard laughed. "No, don't be silly. It's safe."

Charlie let go of Howard's arm. Cautiously he followed Howard onto the small front porch and watched as Howard, with a bit of effort, opened the door. The rusty hinges creaked and groaned in protest.

"I'll have to get some oil for those," Howard said.

Charlie stepped inside. He covered his nose and mouth with his hand while he looked around at the dust that covered everything. The cabin was just one room with a table and four chairs in the center. An old stone fireplace was built into the center of the back wall. Charlie noticed a rocking chair that looked as though it were about to crumble into a pile of sticks was placed close to one side of the fireplace. Against the wall opposite the rocker was a tall cupboard of sorts.

Howard noticed Charlie looking at it. "That's where the brothers kept a few tools," he said. "However, some of the guys used to stash girly magazines in it."

"Really? How did they get those?"

"Beats me."

"Are they still in there?"

"Let's see," Howard said with a grin. He walked over to the cupboard and with a little more effort than he anticipated, opened the doors. A cloud of dust fell from the top, causing Howard to step back while he choked and coughed. Once the dust settled, the boys looked inside. "Nope. Either they burned them before they graduated or the brothers found them and destroyed them."

"Oh," Charlie said. He did not really want to see them. He was more concerned that if the magazines were still there and the brothers found them, Howard and he would get the blame and be in deep trouble. Still, Charlie had to admit he felt a twinge of curiosity.

"This place could use a bit of cleaning, but what do you think? Is this not a cool hangout?" Howard said as he walked around the table.

"Yeah," Charlie nodded. "A lot of cleaning."

"We can borrow a couple brooms and some stuff from the maintenance closet back at the abbey."

"Won't someone miss them?"

"We'll return the stuff. I did say borrow."

"Yeah," Charlie said, still looking around at all of the dust and cobwebs. "What about a light?"

"Well, we can't use a lantern. The brothers are a bit pyrophobic," Howard said with a little laugh.

"Not without good reason," Charlie said, and laughed with his friend.

"We'll need one of those battery lights. I'll ask my dad for one."

"Good deal. We should also get a clock. That way we won't be late for stuff. I have Dougary's old alarm clock. It's wind up so it'll be perfect."

"Great," Howard said. "You two became close last year, at least that's the way it sounded in your letters."

"I wouldn't say that exactly," Charlie answered. "We were on better terms. He really was a different person after his goons were gone."

"I still can't believe he's a postulant."

"Yeah, it's a big change from where he was five years ago."

Howard looked around the room. "We'll have to get the brooms and stuff and come back later. Don't tell Rick."

"Why not?"

"Because, he doesn't need to know everything. This is our spot."

"Okay."

"Promise? No slip-ups."

"Hey, I'm not the one who can't keep a secret," Charlie protested. "But I promise."

"Good," Howard said, with a little laugh in his voice.

The boys walked back onto the front porch and Howard shut the door. Again, it complained. "And some oil," he said as a way to remind himself.

~§~

It was two days before they could steal away again and return to the cabin. With brooms, mop, bucket of water, rags and an oilcan, they stealthily made their way to the chain gate.

"Where do you two think you're going?" a familiar voice behind them asked, startling them both and causing Charlie to drop the alarm clock. Rick Walters nimbly snagged it. "Why do you need a clock?"

"Give me that," Charlie said, trying not to slop the water out of the bucket.

Rick stepped back and held the clock away. "Not so fast. What are you two up to?" He eyed them suspiciously.

"None of your business," Howard said. "Now give him back his clock and go away."

"How about I keep the clock and see what Father Mark

thinks of your stealing all that stuff?"

"We're not stealing it. We're borrowing it," Charlie said.

"Borrowing. Stealing. I wonder if Father Mark will be able to tell the difference."

Charlie looked at Howard. Their shoulders slumped and both sighed in defeat.

"Fine," Howard said through clenched teeth. "We're going to our new hangout."

"Really?" Rick's expression changed to one of waking up on Christmas morning and seeing the presents under the tree. "Where is it?"

"It's in the abandoned orchard," Howard said, lowering his voice to just above a whisper and looking around to be sure no one else was lurking nearby.

"Can I come with you? Obviously, you are going to be doing some cleaning. I could help."

Charlie and Howard exchanged glances. Then Howard put the broom and mop down on the ground. He took the bucket of water from Charlie and put it in Rick's hands while he retrieved the clock.

"Sure, you can bring the bucket, and don't spill any of the water or you'll have to get us some more." He handed the clock back to Charlie before picking up his supplies. "Keep up, Walters."

"Don't worry. I've got it," Rick said, his voice sounding a bit strained as he carried the heavy metal bucket while following the two.

When they reached the cabin, Rick was several yards behind. They waited on the porch for him to catch up.

"This old place?" Rick said, sounding winded.

"Yes," Howard answered. "If you don't like it, you can go."

"No, no," Rick said, setting the bucket down and examining his sore hands. He rubbed the places where the handle left an impression. "It's fine. Are you sure it isn't going to fall down?"

Howard didn't answer, instead he pushed the door open. It creaked loudly.

Rick covered his ears. "Ouch! Give it some oil, quick!"

That brought a grin to Howard's lips. Just to tease Rick, he quickly opened and closed the door some more, making it protest even louder.

"Stop it!" Rick said.

Charlie agreed and Howard relented.

"Come on, there's a lot of work to do, and we don't have a lot of time," Charlie told Rick while he followed Howard into the cabin.

"Can one of you get this bucket? I carried it all the way out here and my hands hurt."

Howard stuck his head out of the doorway, "That would be a no. Get the bucket and get in here."

"Jeez, slave driver," Rick groaned under his breath and gingerly picked up the bucket. "Ow, ow, ow," he complained while he took the few steps into the cabin. He set the bucket down, careful not to slop any more of the water out.

"What is this place?" he asked.

"The old orchard shed. The brothers used it as a break room," Howard answered.

Rick sneezed. "Can we open a window?"

"No!" Howard answered. "If you break the glass, we can't replace it. Just cover your nose and mouth with one of these rags and start sweeping."

For as much as neither of them had wanted to tell Rick about the hangout, Charlie and Howard were both grateful for the extra set of hands when it came to the cleaning. In no time it seemed they had the inside of the cabin dusted, swept out, and mopped.

"Just dump the water out back," Howard said while he continued to oil the hinges on the door.

"Gotcha," Rick said. He wrapped a rag around his hand before picking up the bucket of dirty water.

After Rick was outside, Charlie looked around the cabin. "It's actually looking pretty good," he said. "I'm sorry we had to tell him about it but he sure came in handy."

"Don't want to talk about it," Howard said as he wiggled the door to check for creaks. Hearing a faint one, he applied a bit more oil on the lowest hinge.

"Hey, guys!" Rick shouted from outside. "You've got to see this!"

Charlie and Howard exchanged looks and then hurried to see what all the fuss was.

"What?" Howard said as the two rounded the back of the cabin.

"We have water!" Rick answered, standing beside a metal pipe sticking out of the ground. At the top of the pipe was a faucet. "Look." He gave the handle a turn and dirty, rust colored water spat and sputtered out.

"That's not going to help us. It's dirty," Howard said, belittling the find.

"If we let it run for a bit, it might clear up," Rick said and looked at the water pouring out of the faucet. "See, it's already started to clear."

Charlie looked at the water. It was true. It was becoming cleaner.

"I'm still not going to drink it," Howard said.

"No one said anything about drinking it," Rick said, his tone snippy. "We could use it to clean the mop and stuff. We don't need to lug a bucket of water down here every time we need to clean."

"Fine," Howard said, obviously not wanting to give Rick any credit. He turned around and headed back into the cabin. "Don't forget the bucket, Walters," he shouted over his shoulder.

Charlie watched Rick turn the faucet off and pick up the bucket before he turned around and followed Howard.

Once inside, Howard put the rags and oilcan in the empty bucket and set it by the door. The three then sat down at the table to rest.

"Can you believe our senior year is about to begin?" Rick said.

"No," Howard said, mockingly. "Say it isn't so."

"Knock it off, Miller. Damn, I sure didn't miss you last year," Rick snapped back at him.

"Funny, I didn't miss you either."

"Okay, you two, stop it. We have this last year together before—whatever happens. Let's not spend it bickering with each other," Charlie said. "Let's have fun. We're together again. Too bad Gus couldn't be here."

"Yeah," Howard said quietly.

"What do you hear from him? Anything?" Charlie asked Rick.

Rick shook his head. "I went to see him a couple weeks ago. The nuns told me he wasn't there. He had run away and the police are still looking for him."

"Run away?" Howard said, sitting forward in his chair and looking worried. "Where would he go?"

Rick's expression changed and Charlie knew it meant he was going to make a sarcastic remark. "Rick," he warned between clenched teeth.

Rick's face softened. "Don't know."

"Did he give you any indication? I mean, you two were writing to each other, weren't you?" Howard asked. The concern in his voice was as evident as the tears that were filling his eyes.

"He told me he hated it there. There were some boys there who were worse than Dougary. They were giving him a hard time."

"Didn't the sisters do anything?"

"Apparently not. In the last letter I received, he said he wanted to get away. He thought he would be better off on his own than staying there."

"Did you tell anyone?"

"No. That's why I went to see him. To try to talk to him

and suggest he ask to come back here. But I was too late."

"So now what?" Charlie asked.

"We have to find him," Howard said and slammed his fist down on the table.

"How are we going to find him when the police can't?" Rick asked.

"I don't know, but we have to," Howard answered.

"Maybe we should tell Abbot Ambrose," Charlie suggested.

"What good is that going to do?" Rick asked.

"I don't know, but maybe he would help us? He could take us to town and we could look around?" Charlie said.

"What makes you think he's still around there?" Rick asked.

"Because, when have you known Gus to take risks? He's not going to run off to some city or town where he's never been. He's going to stick with what's familiar, where he feels safe," Charlie said.

"And you think that is here?" Rick asked.

"I do," Charlie said.

"Me, too," Howard added.

"I suppose you're right," Rick said. "But I'm still not convinced we should tell the abbot."

"Me, either," Howard said, siding with Rick. "He might tell us to leave it to the police."

"And Gus isn't about to trust them."

"Maybe you're right," Charlie said as he thought about it some more. "Hey, we're seniors. That means we can sign out to go to town on our own."

"Since when?" Howard said.

"Since last year. Dougary told me he had done it several times."

"What did he do there?"

"I don't know. Maybe saw a movie, looked in stores, what difference does it make?"

"None, just curious," Howard said.

"Well, maybe we could sign up to go tomorrow," Charlie said.

"Sure," Rick agreed.

"What do we do if we find him?" Howard asked. "They'll just send him back to the nuns."

Charlie thought for a moment but nothing he imagined seemed to work. "I don't know. We'll figure it out when we find him."

"You're sure we'll find him," Howard said.

"Yes," Charlie answered. "How long has he been gone?"

Before Rick could answer, the alarm on the clock went off. The three jumped and Charlie silenced it.

"We best be getting back. It's almost time for Vespers," Howard said.

THE RUNAWAY

It felt as though Saturday would never arrive, but two days later, it did. Charlie signed up to leave the hilltop and so did Howard and Rick.

"What do you three plan on doing?" Brother Simon asked when he noticed the three had requested permission to go to town.

"Uh...." Rick said, looking like a deer caught in headlights.

"We're just going to look around," Charlie answered.

"Do a little window shopping," Howard added.

"Window shopping," Brother Simon repeated with a bit of a suspicious grin. "Fine, you may go," he told them. "But be back before Vespers or there will be hell to pay. Is that understood?"

"Yes, Brother Simon," they answered as one. "Thank you, Brother Simon," Howard added as they retreated from his presence back into the hallway.

Charlie closed the door to Brother Simon's office.

"That was scary," Rick said. "I thought for a moment he wasn't going to let us go."

"Nah, I knew he'd let us," Howard said as the three

headed for the stairs.

"Window shopping?" Charlie said. "What on earth possessed you to say that?"

"I don't know, it just popped into my head," Howard said with a shrug of his shoulders. "Besides, I couldn't say we were going to a movie. He'd ask which one. The only one playing downtown is *The Exorcist*, and he would never have allowed that."

"True," Rick agreed.

"Besides, what does it matter? We have permission," Howard said, throwing his arms over Charlie's and Rick's shoulders. "Gus, here we come, buddy."

It did not take long before the boys reached downtown, such as it was. There were only two blocks of shops and restaurants on Main Street and a few behind it on First Street, where the cinema was located.

"You said Gus has been missing for two weeks," Howard said to Rick.

"Yes."

Turning to Charlie, Howard said, "And you're sure he'd come back here."

"I can't say for sure, but the orphanage is only about six and a half miles that way," Charlie answered, pointing south. "Even at his pace, he could make it here."

"I'm still not convinced he'd come back here." Howard repeated.

"Before he left, he had a change of heart and said he would miss the abbey. So, I think he would come back here because it's familiar. Remember, he's not much of a risk taker."

"Well, running away is a huge risk," Rick said.

"True, but he's a scaredy cat. He won't stray from what he knows."

"So, how do we find him?" Howard asked.

"We should start by just walking around, looking down alleys and any place that looks abandoned or run down where a runaway might hide."

"That wouldn't be downtown, then," Rick said. "They keep the town looking nice."

"True, but you know how Gus likes to eat. Perhaps he's getting food from one of the restaurants?"

"With what? Does he have money?" Howard asked.

"I doubt it. But if he's hungry enough, he might get it out of the garbage."

"Oh, that's disgusting," Howard said, and grimaced. "He wouldn't do that."

"He wouldn't run away, either, but he did," Rick said.

"Fine, we'll look behind the restaurants, too," Howard said, giving in.

The boys stayed together as they walked down the sidewalks of Main Street, looking for the way into the alley behind the buildings. Between two buildings there was a three-foot gap that went from the street to the back.

"Hey, what about this?" Howard asked.

"It's possible," Charlie said, and looked around to be sure the coast was clear. "Let's give it a try."

"You first," Rick said hesitantly.

"Fine," Howard said. "And I thought Gus was a chicken."

Howard slipped into the narrow space and Charlie followed close behind. He did not look to see if Rick was following or not. He was too intent on keeping up with Howard, and hoping there were not any rats lurking about.

When they reached the end of the narrow passageway, Howard cautiously peeked to be sure there was no one else around.

"It's clear," he reported. "Come on."

The three stepped back into the sunlight and dusted off their black jackets and slacks.

"So, now what?" Howard asked.

"I suppose we look around and see where the restaurants put their garbage," Charlie said.

Howard frowned. "I hate the thought of Gus eating

garbage."

"Well, don't think about it," Charlie said.

"Hey, look there," Rick said, pointing at the street at the end of the alley. "We could have just walked around the corner instead of squeezing between two buildings."

"As if you had to squeeze," Howard said. "None of us were pressed against the walls."

"Why don't we split up and look around," Charlie suggested. "Rick, you take the right and head toward the road. Howard and I will go this other way."

"Why do you two get to be together?"

"Because, that's just the way it is," Howard answered in a tone that dared Rick to object.

Rick did not. He huffed and turned away.

"Come on, Charlie," Howard said.

As they walked, Charlie noticed the garbage cans of the toy store, card shop, and finally one from the restaurant that served German sausages and sauerkraut. The sour smell of rotting cabbage caused Charlie to gag.

"He wouldn't eat this stuff, would he?" he asked Howard.

"I would hope not but—we have to find him."

When they reached the end of the alley, there was no sign that Gus had been there. They regrouped and headed for the alley between Main Street and First.

"We should have brought some paper and a marker," Rick said.

"What for?" Howard asked.

"To make a sign. Let Gus know we're looking for him."

"And then the police would be looking for us," Howard said. "They would want to know if we have seen him or know where he is."

"So, would that be so bad?" Rick asked.

"You're the one who said Gus wouldn't trust them."

"I think Rick is right. We should make some signs. We could be vague enough so only Gus would recognize what it says. I've got some money. Maybe we could buy what we need, but where would we leave them?" Charlie asked.

"Where did you get money? Your grandma?" Howard asked.

"No—I mean, yeah," Charlie answered, realizing his slip. "So, what do you think?"

"We could leave it in the alley behind restaurants," Rick said.

"Sounds like we have a plan."

The boys headed to the stationary shop on First Street across from the theatre. The store was larger than Charlie expected, though he did not really know what he imagined. He had never been in an actual store that sold stuff like the abbey's little shop in the basement. There were four aisles, two to the right and two to the left, with a center aisle that led to the cash register in the back. The aisles ran from the front to the back of the store with shelves on either side. An older woman with gray hair in a braid that went from ear-to-ear over the top of her head, looked up from the register.

"Good afternoon, boys," she greeted them with a smile. "Is there something I can help you find?"

"We're just looking," Howard said, which earned him a glare from Rick.

"Actually," Charlie spoke up. "We're looking for something to make a couple signs. Maybe a marker and some paper."

"Is the sign for indoors or outside?" the shopkeeper asked.

"Outside."

"Then you would want to use posterboard. It's stronger and will hold up to the weather a bit better than lightweight paper. I'll show you," she said and flipped a piece of the counter up like the trap door in the belfry. She opened a little gate on the front of the counter and walked into the main part of the store. "This way boys," she said, and led the way to the wall on the left. "We have all sorts of colors."

"Well, I was thinking about just white," Charlie said.

"White it is, then. How many posters do you need to make?"

Charlie glanced at Howard and Rick who both just shrugged their shoulders in reply. "I think maybe four will do it, but they only need to be about this big." He held up his hands and gestured about the size of a piece of notebook paper.

"Very well," the woman said. "I can cut this one sheet down for you if you like?"

"That would be great."

"Now, you'll need a marker," she said and walked away. Charlie and the others quickly followed her to the opposite side of the store. "What color would you like? We have them all."

Again, Howard and Rick were no help. "Just black," Charlie answered. "We just want to make a sign for a friend."

"A friend?" she asked and cocked her head.

"Well," Charlie stammered and cringed. He glanced at Howard and Rick. They both looked shocked and scared, but remained mute. Charlie turned back to the shopkeeper. "Yes, he ran away from school."

"From the abbey?" The woman sounded shocked and surprised.

"No, not the abbey," Charlie said. He had already said too much; he might as well spill it all. "He ran away from the orphanage."

"Oh, that place."

The shopkeeper's tone surprised Charlie.

"You haven't seen a chubby boy with blond hair and blue eyes wandering around, have you?"

"Come to think of it, I may have. When did he run away?" she asked as she returned to her station behind the cash register. She lay the pen and posterboard down on the counter.

"About two weeks ago, isn't that right, Rick?"

"Yes," Rick answered.

"Well, that sounds about right," she said, nodding her

head. "Yes, I think I might have."

"You're kidding! Really?" Howard said, and stepped forward. "Where? When?"

The shopkeeper smiled. "It was the day before yesterday. I was on my lunch break and about to go into The Village Haus on Main Street when I noticed a somewhat pudgy young man with blond hair who looked a little scruffy. He was talking with a man on the corner so I paid him no more mind and went inside. Do you think that could have been him?"

"It might," Charlie said. "We thought if we put up signs to let him know we were looking for him he might contact us."

"Have you considered calling the police and letting them know he might be here? Someone will be worried."

Charlie swallowed hard. "Yes, the police already know. We just wanted to help."

"We figured he might trust us," suggested Howard.

She nodded

"Well, I'll just go in back and cut it up for you."

"Thank you," Charlie said as she disappeared into the back room.

"What did you go and tell her all that for?" Rick snapped at Charlie.

"Why? Didn't you hear what she said? She saw him!"

"But now she knows he's a runaway. Do you really think she believed you guys are working with the police? She'll never buy it. She'll tell the police," Rick protested, not concerned about the volume of his voice.

"That's okay, I'm not going to tell the police," the woman said, suddenly appearing behind the cash register with the four pieces of posterboard.

"Oh," Rick said, looking shocked. "Why?"

"I wouldn't send a dog to that orphanage."

Now it was the boys' turn to be surprised. "Why's that?" Howard asked.

"Because I've heard too many stories about what goes on with the children there. How the nuns are too strict with them. Sometimes they bring a few boys with them for school supplies, and I've seen my share of bruises and scratches. The sisters usually say they fell down, but I think they are mistreating them."

"Our friend ran away because he was being bullied by some of the other boys," Rick said.

"Well, I'm not surprised. That sort of environment can't help but create bullies," she said and slid the pen and paper toward Charlie.

"How much do I owe you?" he asked.

"Nothing."

"Really?"

"Yes," she answered with a smile. "I hope you find your friend, and if I see him, can I give him a message for you?"

Charlie looked at Howard and Rick. "Sure," he answered. "Do you have a piece of paper and a pen?"

"You do know what kind of store this is," she answered with a laugh as she took a tablet from beneath the counter and a pen and handed it to him.

"Sorry," Charlie said. He quickly wrote a note to Gus, telling him about the cabin and to go there. "Can we put on the poster for him to see you? That way you can give him this message."

"Sure, I would be happy to help."

After Charlie finished the note and posters, they thanked the shopkeeper and headed for the door.

"Here," she called to them. "You'll need something to hang the posters with. Here are some tacks." She handed Rick a package of sixteen brass thumbtacks.

"Thank you, again," Charlie said before leaving the shop.

"I can't believe our luck," Howard said.

"What luck? I told you he'd come back here," Rick said, his haughty tone returning.

"So, what did you put in the note?" Howard asked.

"I told him how to find the cabin," Charlie answered.

"What!" Howard exclaimed, looking shocked and a bit angry at Charlie.

"It was the only place I could think of. I mean, I couldn't tell him to walk through the front doors of the abbey, could I?"

"No, but—oh, never mind. We'll figure out what to do if he ever shows up."

After hanging the posters near the garbage cans in back of the restaurants, the boys took another look around the streets but did not see anyone who looked like Gus. It was getting late, so they headed back to the abbey.

SENIORS

Sunday morning the boys gathered in their fourth-floor chapel for Mass. Charlie selected Howard and Rick to serve the Mass with him.

"After Mass, Rick, I'd like you to carry the thurible and incense boat—"

"Why can't Howard? I always have to do it," Rick protested. "I have allergies and the smoke gets in my face and I end up smelling the incense for days."

"Howard is going to carry the holy water bucket and aspergillum," Charlie explained.

Howard picked up the shiny brass pail that resembled a chalice but with a deeper bowl and a handle, and what looked like a large baby rattle. He dipped the round ball end into the holy water and then flicked it at Rick.

"Knock it off, Howard!" Rick snapped and wiped the water from his face. "Charlie, come on. Let Howard have the incense this time."

"I could ask another member to serve in your place, if you want?"

Rick thought for a moment. "No, I'll do it," he said begrudgingly.

"Now, after Father Mark concludes the Mass, we are going to form a procession down to the second floor. I will go first with the cross. You two will walk side by side after me followed by Father Mark and then Father Vicar. We will walk slowly so the student body can get in line behind us. When we reach the second floor, we will stop outside the fire doors and Father Vicar will offer a prayer. Then he will proceed inside, where everyone will wait by the door. Father Vicar will first walk down the hall sprinkling holy water and then he will return waving the thurible, blessing the school and praying for a good year. When they are finished, the three of us will come back here and change back into our uniforms. Questions?"

"No, I got it," Rick said, still sounding upset.

At the close of the Mass, Charlie took his place with the processional cross in front of the altar. Rick collected the thurible and incense boat. He stood behind Charlie's right shoulder. Howard, holy water bucket in hand, took his place behind Charlie's left shoulder. The three walked slowly down the aisle toward the door. The incense smoke bellowed into Rick's face, just as expected. He turned his head but the smoke kept finding his face. Finally, he switched hands and held the chain of the thurible in his left hand so the smoke would find Howard instead. Howard glared at Rick when the smoke wafted into his face. He took a step away and the smoke returned to Rick.

"Boys," Father Mark's voice, though slightly above a whisper, reverberated.

Charlie did not dare turn his head to see what was happening behind him. Instead, he continued to walk toward the chapel door. Once in the hallway, he turned right and headed for the stairs at the opposite end of the student wing. The smell of the incense reassured him that the others were following as they should.

Once Charlie reached the second floor landing, he stepped to the side to let Howard, Rick, Father Mark, and Father Vicar have access to the fire doors. Several of the boys crowded on the landing while the others backed up on the stairs.

Father Vicar offered his prayer and then turned around to face the doors. Howard took hold of the one door and glanced at Rick who looked panicked since both his hands were occupied. Rick handed Father Mark the incense boat and then grabbed the door handle. The boys pulled the doors open and tripped the doorstop latch to hold them in place. Rick held out his hand to take back the incense boat but Father Mark motioned for him to open the thurible instead. After adding a fresh spoonful of incense to the burning charcoal ember, Rick coughed and closed the thurible. He traded it with Father Mark for the boat.

As Father Vicar and Father Mark made their way down the hallway, Howard and Rick followed closely behind. When they returned, Father Vicar addressed the boys.

"As we do at the beginning of each school year, we will now begin the tour of your classrooms. The tour will be conducted by each grade. The seniors will be guided by Father Mark. The juniors, by Brother Simon. Sophomores, Brother Conrad, and the freshmen will go with Brother Owen. No one is to wander off alone. Your tour will not proceed until all members of your grade are present. Is that understood?"

"Yes, Father Vicar," the boys said loudly. Their voices amplified and echoed in the stairwell.

"Very well," Father Vicar said. "You may form your lines."

Father Vicar turned to Charlie and the other altar boys. "Let's use the other stairs." He turned around and led the three down the hallway toward the staircase in the center of the abbey above the main foyer.

After the three boys changed back into their blazers, they quickly headed back to the second floor. Father Mark stood patiently waiting with the other nine seniors. Once everyone was present, he began the tour.

"We will start with your home room," he said and led the boys down the hallway to the left of the fire doors. "This first room," he said, motioning to the door to his left, "is the restroom."

Charlie noticed the sign that said as much attached to the door.

"This next room is the freshmen class's homeroom. Across from it is the sophomore's," he said as he continued down the hall. He motioned again to his left. "Juniors." He stopped and when he reached the last door on the right. "This is your home room," he said and opened the door. He held it and let the boys enter before following them.

"Go ahead," he instructed. "The desks have already been assigned. You will find your nameplate on the front of your desk."

To the left of the door was mounted a chalkboard that spanned the wall to the corner. In front of the chalkboard and facing into the room was one of the large metal desks from their previous classrooms in the basement. Brand new desks with wooden tops that raised to reveal a metal tub-like space beneath for storing books and other supplies were arranged into four rows of three. Behind them was the wall with windows that overlooked the abbey church wing in the center of the abbey building. Beneath the windows and spanning the wall was a bookcase filled with reference books and other supplies.

Charlie found his desk in the middle of the second row from the door. Howard was behind him. Rick's desk was two rows over, against the wall furthest from the door and in the back beneath the windows.

"Each morning you will meet here. The majority of your classes will be held in this classroom. Now that you are all seated, please stand up and follow." Father Mark returned to the hallway. The boys scrambled to catch up.

When they reached the fire doors, Father Mark directed their attention to the office in front of them. "This is Father Vicar's office. For any new students, he is our school's principal."

Turning down the main hallway, he motioned to the

next door. "This is Brother Owen's office. He's the vice-principal. Next door to his office is the teachers' lounge and next to it, the book room. You pick up your school books here and return them at year's end. The door across the hall here is the biology lab. Then we have the chemistry lab and finally the typing room at the end, on the left. Over here, on this side of the hallway next to the bookroom is the yearbook office, journalism room, and the learning center. The band will use the back room in the gymnasium and the choir will meet for the time being in the choir room in the basement. Any questions? Yes, Master Walters?"

"When do we sign up for classes?"

"You should have already done so," Father Mark said. "It was in the registration packet we sent to your parents last summer. If you need to sign up or check your classes, you may see Brother Owen or Father Vicar. Yes, Master Walters."

"Can we switch classes if we don't like, say choir?"

"You need to take either choir or band, so if you want to switch, see Brother Owen or Father Vicar," Father Mark said and scanned the boys for any more questions. He consulted his clipboard. "To keep things running smoothly, your class has been assigned to pick up your books at three this afternoon." He glanced at his wristwatch. "That's in thirty minutes. You may want to hang out here and look around until then. This concludes the tour."

"Thank you, Father Mark," the boys said.

Charlie turned to Howard. "Let's go check out the homeroom again."

They headed back down the side hall.

"Did you notice how Rick slithered over to the book room door while Father Mark was talking?" Howard asked.

"Yeah," Charlie said with a laugh. "He always has to be the first in line."

"I don't really care. I'll still get my books no matter if I'm first or last."

"True," Charlie agreed.

The boys entered their homeroom and sat down at their desks.

"So, what do you think of this place?" Charlie asked.

"They did a good job. I can't smell any smoke." Howard said and sniffed the air. "Hard to believe there was ever a fire on this floor."

"True. I hope there isn't another one, at least not while I'm still here."

"Agreed. That was a horrible year. I was getting nervous they were going to blame me for it. I kept failing those polygraph tests."

"I'm just glad they figured it out and kicked DeVries out," Charlie said. "So, who do you think our homeroom teacher will be?"

"I don't really care who it is. Since Father Vicar's principal, it won't be him, so that's all that matters," Howard said and raised the top of his desk to look inside.

Charlie looked out the window and his thoughts turned to Gus. "Do you think Gus will see our signs?"

Howard closed his desk. "I don't know. If he does, he'll have to wait until tomorrow before he can find that lady at the stationary store."

"Gee, I hope he does."

"Then what is the plan? I mean, he can't live in the cabin forever."

"I know. I was wondering if he does show up, maybe I could talk to Abbot Ambrose about him. See if he'll let Gus stay and go to school with us?"

"That would be too cool, but I don't think he will."

"It's worth a try."

"Well, first let's see if Gus even shows up before we tip our hand."

~§~

At breakfast the next morning, the excitement in the

refectory was deafening. Several times, Father Mark had to silence the boys by pounding on the block of wood on the head table. Finally, they quieted down and finished their meal. After the usual announcements about making sure their beds were neatly made before class or risk receiving work crew, no running in the halls, and do not be late to class, the boys were excused until Mass in the chapel.

Father Mark offered Mass. His abbreviated sermon was on honesty. Howard kept falling asleep. Twice Charlie had to nudge him to keep him from falling out of his chair. After putting away the vestments and securing Father Mark's chalice in the locker they used as a safe, Charlie and Howard headed to their homeroom.

The teacher was not there when they entered and took their seats. Charlie glanced at Rick, who was carefully crafting a book cover for his Modern Problems text book out of a brown paper sack. He motioned for Howard to take a look.

"He's afraid of it getting damaged," Howard said. "If it gets damaged, he loses his book fee."

"Hey, Miller," the boy seated in front of Rick said.

"What do you want, Turner?" Howard answered.

"I heard a rumor that Brother Ichabod is going to be our home room teacher."

"Don't be ridiculous. He retired from teaching regular school a long time ago."

"Well, that's what I heard."

"Don't believe everything you hear," Howard said and turned back to Charlie. "So, you got a letter from your grandma this morning?"

"Yes," Charlie answered.

"Did she have much to say?"

"Not really. Just her usual pep talk stuff. She did say that my uncle has been by several times in the last week, which is odd. He hasn't paid that much attention to her since he dumped her in that home."

"I wonder what he wants."

"I think I know, but he's not getting it."

"What?"

The sound of a monk entering the room made Charlie turn back toward the front of the classroom.

"Oh crap!" Howard whispered.

"Good morning, class," Father Vicar said as he stood, back straight, nose in the air.

"Good morning, Father Vicar," they all responded, out of sync with each other and creating an echo effect which brought a scowl from the principal.

"Let's try that again," he said. "All together."

"Good morning, Father Vicar," they said in unison. Charlie fought the urge to add an extra Vicar to the end and the thought made him nearly laugh.

"Your homeroom teacher is running late this morning, but he will be here momentarily. Until then, I will be filling in. Take out your schedules and we will review what is happening today."

The boys complied.

When Father Vicar was finished reviewing the boys' schedule, the classroom door opened. A young monk with thinning dark brown hair and round, wire-rimmed eyeglasses entered. Charlie recognized him immediately.

"I'm sorry I'm late," he said to the principal.

Father Vicar's back straightened and he looked down his nose at the monk. "See that it doesn't happen again."

"Yes, Father," he said, and waited while Father Vicar gathered his papers and left the room. Once the door clicked shut, he let out a sigh and shook his head. He hoisted his briefcase and dropped it on top of the desk. "Well, seems like I'm starting off on the wrong foot," he said to the class. "Is he always like that?"

"Yes," Howard answered. "And worse, if that were possible."

Howard's comment brought a grin to the monk's lips and a twinkle in his brown eyes. He withdrew a sheet of paper from his briefcase and walked around to the front of his desk. To the surprise of the boys, he jumped up and sat on the desk, letting his feet dangle beneath his habit.

"My name is Brother Linus. I'll be your homeroom teacher for this year. I'll give you a little bit of information about myself. I graduated from Juilliard in New York. I had a career on Broadway for a time, and then received my calling. I joined the Order in Idaho, of all places. Went from the big city to the middle of nowhere." He laughed and the boys laughed with him.

"That brings me to you." He stretched out his arms and opened his hands, palms up, toward the boys for a moment. Then he lowered them and clasped the edge of the desktop on either side of his legs. He leaned forward slightly while he continued. "This year will go by quickly, but it is the most important year of your young lives. You are at a crossroads where you are leaving your childhood behind and becoming adults. You are going to be asked to make a lot of weighty decisions this year that will affect your futures. Will you pursue higher education or will you decide to enter the workforce? If you decide on education, where? What will you study and with what goal in mind? If you opt for the workplace, what sort of work interests you? Or maybe for some of you, you will pursue a religious calling. My advice to each of you is, take this year very seriously and give it a lot of prayerful thought, but keep in mind, your future is not etched in stone. Even if you decide on one route, it doesn't mean you can't take another later. I am proof of that."

Charlie listened with keen interest, especially the part about New York. He wondered if Brother Linus knew any of the O'Sullivans, but then, he looked too young, and New York was huge.

When the bell rang for the boys to get ready for their first class, Charlie turned around in his chair to face Howard.

"I like him," he said.

"Me, too." Howard agreed.

"Hey, we should check the cabin after lunch," he

whispered.

"There's not enough time," Howard said. "Besides, what good would it do? If he's there, he can hang out until after classes."

"True," Charlie said.

"Master MacCready, turn around," Sister Mary Anthony said as she took her place at the head of the classroom. "Good morning, class," she greeted them with a smile. "For those of you who do not know me, my name is Sister Mary Anthony. This year we will expose you to American authors such as Nathaniel Hawthorne, Joseph Heller, Ernest Hemingway, Edgar Allen Poe, J. D. Salinger, John Steinbeck, and Mark Twain. Some we will just introduce you to, but others, we will take the time to get to know better."

Charlie did not like the sound of that last part. He knew what it meant, reading. He was not a fast reader and after an embarrassing moment in last year's Classic English Lit class when he was the only one to miss the one question on the test about the book they were assigned to read, he was not looking forward to a repeat. Still, he forced himself to stay focused and in the present, and not allow his mind to wander too far.

After the final bell rang, Charlie ditched his books in his desk and joined Howard on the front steps. The two headed for the cabin.

"Do you think he'll be there?" Charlie asked.

"How would I know?" Howard said. "I hope he is but—oh, crap!"

"Howard!" Charlie chastised him before he saw Rick standing in front of the chained off road. "Dang!"

"Hi, guys," Rick greeted in a cheery tone. "You gonna go to the hangout?"

"Maybe," Howard answered.

"Think Gus will be there?"

"Keep your voice down," Howard said, ducking his head and looking over his shoulder toward the abbey. "Do you want to have one of the brothers hear you?"

"I wasn't talking that loudly," Rick whispered.

"Yeah, well, your sissy voice carries."

"Watch it, Miller," Rick said. "I can still go to Father Mark about the cabin."

"No one's stopping you, Walters."

"Guys, come on, enough," Charlie interrupted. "Let's just get to the cabin and see."

"Fine," Howard said and stepped over the chain.

Charlie quickly followed while Rick slipped around the end post.

"God, I hope he's there," Howard said as the three walked side by side along the overgrown rutted road.

"Then what's the plan?" Rick asked.

"I don't know. We'll just have to wait and see what he wants to do," Howard said, beginning to sound worried.

"Well, whatever the case, he's going to be hungry," Rick continued. "We'll need to get him something to eat, but how?"

"I might have an idea," Charlie said, thinking about Sister Faith in the kitchen.

"Might?" Howard said. "You either have an idea or don't. You can't almost have a thought." He laughed.

"Well, I haven't figured out all of the details yet," Charlie said.

When they reached the cabin, to their dismay, there was no sign of Gus. After walking around back and searching the orchard as far as they dared, they returned to their hangout and went inside. Charlie wound the alarm clock and set it to go off in plenty of time for them to make it to Vespers.

"Now what do we do?" Rick asked, sounding antsy.

"We wait and see," Howard said.

"Well, I've got homework to do, I can't just sit around here."

"No one is keeping you."

Rick glared at Howard again. "That does it. I'm outta here. Let me know if he shows up."

"Maybe."

"We will," Charlie said and shook his head at Howard.

When Rick left the cabin he slammed the door, causing Charlie to jump. It caused the medal, key, and locket to tink beneath his shirt. He quickly put his hand over them.

"So, did you ever figure out what that key was for? You left off mentioning it when you said your cousin paid the Muster twins to steal it."

Charlie felt his anxiety begin to stir. He looked at his hands and noticed them start to tremble.

"Ah-ha!" Howard said. "You did!"

Charlie looked surprised. "No, I didn't."

"Yes, you did."

"How do you know?"

"Because you're a rotten liar. You always look away before you start to lie."

Charlie's shoulders slumped. He remembered how he told Howard about the key even though he promised his grandmother he would not tell anyone. Howard kept his secret and nothing too awful happened, really. He let out a heavy sigh.

"Fine," he said. "But you cannot, and I mean it, cannot tell a soul."

"Cross my heart and hope you die," Howard said.

"It's hope to die, not hope you die," Charlie corrected.

"You say it how you want, and I'll say it how I want," Howard laughed.

"Oh," Charlie said and shuddered. "Fine. After catching my cousin, Abbot Ambrose had me come into a sitting room where my grandmother was waiting. In the center of the room was the trunk from Saint Nicholas dorm."

"I thought you said you tried that lock."

"I did and it didn't fit," Charlie answered. "But inside the truck was a smaller box. The key fit the lock on it."

Howard's eyes widened and his mouth gaped. "That trunk has been in that dorm for as long as I have been here. You mean, your box was inside it the whole time?"

Charlie shrugged. "I suppose."

"So, what was in the box?"

Charlie hesitated and started to look at his hands but remembered what Howard had said about him lying. "It had these small gold pieces and a lot of old money."

"Money? How much?"

"I don't know. But it also came with a letter."

"A letter?"

"Yes, from my grandfather on my dad's side. It was addressed to the abbot back when my grandparents sent him to live here. He was a little boy at the time."

"Wow. That's amazing."

"Not really," Charlie said, feeling his mood sink into the pit of his stomach.

"What's the matter?"

"My grandfather signed it Danny O'Sullivan."

"Why did he do that?"

"Because that was his name."

"What about MacCready?"

"That was the name the abbot back then gave my dad."

Howard looked a bit confused. "Why would he do that?"

"Because, according to the letter, my grandfather sent my dad here to hide him from the Irish Mafia."

Howard laughed.

"What's so funny?"

"You're joking, right?"

"No. I'm serious. I don't understand it all but that's what it said. That's also why my parents left me with my grandma."

"Okay, I'm confused. Why would they do that?"

"I don't know. Something about someone trying to get the box from my dad and threatening to let it out who my dad really is."

"Wow! How bizarre," Howard said. By the look on his face, Charlie was not convinced Howard believed him. He was not even sure he believed it. "So, what's next? Find your parents?"

"No."

"No?" Howard repeated and raised his voice. "Why on earth not? I mean, ever since you came here all I have heard is 'I'm not an orphan. Someday my parents will come for me.'"

"Well, they didn't. Now, Father Cecil thinks I should be focusing on what I want to do with my life."

"What does he know?" Howard said dismissively. "I say, after we graduate, we should track them down. Find out why they didn't come for you like they promised."

Charlie shook his head. "Over the summer I talked to Father Ignatius. He said it would be near impossible to find someone who doesn't want to be found. And, they don't want to be found. Besides, it doesn't matter anymore. We'll never be the family I had imagined. I mean, I can't go back to being a little kid. No. I think Father Cecil is right. I should move on. To hell with them."

Howard's mouth dropped open. After a bit, he spoke. "I'm not giving up on the idea of us taking a road trip."

"Now who's being funny."

"I mean it."

"And where would we get a car?"

"Don't worry about that. I'll figure that part out," Howard said.

The alarm clock went off, causing both boys to jump and laugh. Charlie turned it off and made sure it was wound. He placed the clock on the wooden mantle above the fireplace.

ANOTHER GHOST STORY

The sun felt warm against Charlie's face as he sat with Father Cecil by the pond on the Great Lawn. The goldfish occasionally broke the surface of the water leaving behind tiny bubbles.

"How was your first week of school?" Father Cecil asked.

"It was okay, I guess. We already had a test in Father Vicar's Modern Problems class."

"Really? So soon?"

"Yes. He had us watch a movie and then we had to answer twenty-seven questions. If we had even one wrong, he said we would receive a failing grade."

"How did you do?"

"I failed."

"How bad?"

"I missed the last question."

"I'm so sorry."

"I don't care. I'm not trying to please him. I know I did okay and one wrong answer out of twenty-seven is ninety-six percent correct. In any other class that would have been an A."

"True."

"I don't know why he has to be such a jerk," Charlie said, staring at the goldfish swimming beneath the surface of the water.

"A jerk, son?"

"Sorry," Charlie said. "But, that's how I feel. I don't understand why Abbot Ambrose appointed him principal. He hates kids. He's had it in for me since I came here. I've heard some of the stuff he's said."

"I can't argue with that, but you mustn't call him or anyone else names," Father Cecil said. "It only lowers you to their level."

"I guess you're right. I'm sorry."

"You're forgiven, son. So, tell me, are you happy to have Master Miller back?"

"Yes. Father Mark even made him a member of the Altar Boys Club again. He's assigned to a new brother. I think Father Christopher."

"Oh, they should do just fine. Tell me, what else have you been up to?"

"Well," Charlie said, and then thought for a moment.

"And?"

"Howard, Rick, and I have a new hangout since Abbot Ambrose and Father Mark said the belfry is off limits."

"Oh? Is it a secret?"

"Well, sort of. I mean, we're not telling the other boys. It's a little rundown cabin in the middle of the old orchard."

"Ah, the old cabin," Father Cecil said, nodding and smiling. "There are stories about the old cabin. Perhaps you heard one of them?"

Charlie thought for a moment. "No. I don't think I have. Tell me."

"Well, many, many years ago, we had an old brother who was the caretaker of the orchard. He had worked there for years and really enjoyed it. Under his nurturing, the trees produced tons of apples. Then one day, he didn't show up for Vespers or for dinner. When it was determined he hadn't returned from the orchard, two brothers were sent to find him. They found him in the cabin, sitting in the rocking chair by the fire."

"What was wrong? Did he say why he missed prayer and dinner?"

Father Cecil's lips curled into a sympathetic smile. "No, son. He had died."

"Oh my," Charlie gasped and shuddered. He looked away from the pond, toward the gym. He had sat down in that chair a couple times. The thought of sitting in a dead man's chair gave him goosebumps and creeped him out.

"What's the matter?" Father Cecil asked.

"Nothing. It's just so sad," Charlie lied.

"Indeed, it must have been, I'm sure. I wasn't here then, so I'm just guessing. By my time, the boys had built up a ghost story of sorts about the incident. How after his death the trees were so grieved they stopped growing apples and their branches became gnarled. One story said he still walks the orchard at night, chanting to the trees. And, yet another said that the rocking chair will suddenly start rocking for no apparent reason. It's all just boyish nonsense," Father Cecil said with a slight laugh in his voice.

Charlie did not believe in ghosts, but knowing that someone actually died in that cabin and seeing the condition of the orchard, he felt a bit of fear stir deep inside of him.

"You okay?" Father Cecil asked.

"Yeah, I guess so. Crazy stories. Howard told me one when I first came here. It was about the ghost in the attic. Turned out to be Dougary's adoptive father."

"Yes, I remember that. I'm happy he didn't hurt you."

"Me, too." Charlie laughed.

"So, I heard you went to town for the day last weekend. How did that go?" Father Cecil changed the subject.

"Oh, all right, I guess."

"What did you do?"

"We just did some window shopping. That's what

Howard calls looking at stuff and don't buying anything."

"You said 'we'. Does that mean Master Miller went with you?"

"Yes. Rick also went along."

"Oh, I see. What do you think of the little town?"

"It's small. Sort of like the town where I lived with my grandma. It was small, too. Rick calls it quaint, but I don't think he meant it as a compliment. Oh, the lady who works at the stationary shop was really nice."

"You talked to her?"

"Yeah, we needed some paper and a pen to make a post—" Charlie stopped himself, realizing that he had said too much.

"A poster?" Father Cecil asked. "Why did you need to make a poster?"

"I can't tell you," Charlie said, feeling a bit uneasy keeping a secret from his friend.

"Can't or won't?"

"I promised Howard and Rick I wouldn't say anything."

"I see. Well, if you promised, I won't press it."

"Thank you."

After concluding his visit with Father Cecil and safely returning him to his room, Charlie headed for the cabin. Howard and he had made arrangements to meet there after they finished their Altar Boys Club duties.

While Charlie walked along the overgrown gravel road to the cabin, the words of Father Cecil kept coming to mind and with them a bit of trepidation. He looked over his shoulder several times hoping to see Howard, but he did not.

With the cabin in view, Charlie stopped. He looked back again for Howard but there was still no sign of him. He looked at the cabin. It did not appear to be occupied, but then without going inside he really could not tell.

"Oh, quit being stupid," Charlie chastised himself. "There is no such thing as ghosts. Besides, why would a holy monk haunt his former abbey?" With renewed determination, he marched up to the cabin door. He reached for the doorknob and gave it a turn.

"There you are!" Howard said from behind Charlie.

Charlie jumped and let out a scream that echoed across the butte. "Don't do that!" Charlie said with his hand over his racing heart.

Howard was too busy laughing to hear. Charlie slugged him on the shoulder. "Ow!" Howard said, rubbing the sting away. "Why are you so jumpy?"

Embarrassed by letting his fear get the better of him, Charlie did not answer. Instead, he opened the door and went inside. He took one step and stopped.

Looking around the room, Charlie noticed that the rocking chair had been moved to the corner behind the door. The clock he had left on the mantle was now on the table. There were also unburned twigs in the fireplace. Charlie turned toward Howard. "Have you been down here?"

"No," he answered and walked around Charlie. He looked at the cabin and noticed the same things Charlie had. "Who—"

"Maybe Rick has been here," Charlie said in an attempt to calm his growing fears.

"Rick wouldn't come out here on his own. It's too far of a walk to sit in an empty room."

"True."

"That means it must have been Gus," Charlie said, feeling excited. He looked through the window at the orchard but only saw the bent and gnarled branches of the old apple trees. Fear once again swept over him as he remembered what Father Cecil had said. He shuddered.

Charlie grabbed the rocking chair and dragged it across the wooden floor to where he found it originally, beside the fireplace. He then picked the clock to wind it but noticed it had already been wound. With hands that were starting to tremble, he put it back on the mantle.

"What's the matter with you?" Howard asked. "Why

are you so jumpy?"

"Oh, it's nothing. Just some dumb story Father Cecil told me about the cabin this afternoon."

Again, Howard laughed. "Oh, the old monk and the orchard story."

Charlie's eyes widened in surprise. "You know about that?"

"Yes, everyone does."

"Well, not everyone," Charlie said, sounding a bit annoyed by Howard's continued laughter.

"I thought you didn't believe in ghosts," Howard managed to say.

"I don't," Charlie said.

The sound of footsteps outside on the wooden porch silenced the boys. Quickly and quietly, they huddled together in the corner behind the door. Slowly it opened and the visitor stepped inside. The door closed.

"Gus!" they shouted.

Gus let out a scream and stumbled as he took a step away from them. He still looked much the same as when Charlie had seen him last, though his haircut was a better style. Not so much like someone put a bowl on his head and cut around it. Gus was a bit taller, but then so was Howard and he. Gus looked thinner, possibly due to lack of eating for the last couple weeks. The boys rushed him and gave him a hug.

"You found our posters," Howard said.

"Stop it. You're breaking my ribs," Gus groaned and wiggled out of Howard's bear hug. "Yes, I saw them. How did you know I'd be there?"

"Charlie knew actually. He said you'd return to what was familiar," Howard said. "Come on, sit down."

The boys sat down at the table.

"So, how long have you been here?" Charlie asked.

"I snuck up here Wednesday night, when everyone was at dinner."

"Oh," Charlie said feeling guilty remembering that was

the night they had pork chops, mashed potatoes and gravy, green beans and fresh dinner rolls for dinner. Gus's favorites.

"What have you been eating?" Howard asked.

"I had a biscuit the lady in the stationary shop gave me yesterday."

"Well, we'll fix that, won't we, Charlie."

"Yes," Charlie said. "It'll have to wait until after dinner, though. Is that okay?"

"Sure."

"So, why did you run away?" Howard asked.

"I couldn't take another day in that prison," Gus said. "The gestapo—that's what we call the nuns—were mean. It was like they hated us. They kept calling us vile perverts and other horrible names. I don't think they like boys."

"Surely they all weren't like that," Charlie said in their defense.

"No, but the ones in charge of us were. You think Father Vicar is evil. You haven't met Sister Mary Reagan. I swear her head could swivel around."

"That can't be her real name," Howard laughed.

"No, but it should be. The woman is the devil incarnate," Gus said. "She hounded a guy in the senior class last year so bad all year that he tried to hang himself."

"Really?" Charlie gasped.

"Yes. He's okay, though. Some of his classmates found him and quickly cut him down. It was awful. He's now in the state mental hospital. They're wicked, I tell you.

"After that, she started in on me because I couldn't keep up in gym class. All summer she had me doing laps around the track. If I got tired or winded, she would hit me with a switch." He stretched arm out over the table. "See this," he said, pointing at his forearm. "She did this in class with a ruler."

Charlie looked at Gus' arm but saw nothing—no scar, mark, or anything. He looked at Howard and knew that he had not seen anything either.

"I had to get out of there or she would have killed me,"

Gus said. "Living on the streets is preferable to that sort of treatment. I'll never go back."

"Well, you can stay here," Howard said. "We'll figure out how to get some blankets and even a pillow for you. But you can't use the light at night. If you do, one of the monks might see it and come to investigate."

"I know," Gus said. "Gosh, it is so good to see you guys again." He stretched out his arms and put a hand on their shoulders.

"Same here," Charlie said.

"Ditto," Howard added.

Charlie looked at the clock. "Well, we have to get back. Vespers, you know. We'll come back after dinner. I'll bring you something to eat."

"Thanks, guys," Gus said.

Heading back to the abbey, Charlie felt excited and worried at the same time.

"You know, he can't stay there forever," he said to Howard.

"I know, but he can't go back to that place. He'll just run away again and if he does, he's not going to trust us," Howard said.

"I wish there were some way he could stay and go to school with us."

"That would take a miracle," Howard said.

CAUGHT

The aroma in the bakery smelled like heaven to Charlie. He took a deep breath and almost forgot why he had snuck into the room in the first place. Looking around to be sure the coast was clear, he scooted around the end of the kneading table to the large plastic bins used to store the pastries. He opened the first bin and his mouth began to water. He quickly took two apple fritters and placed them in the paper bag he brought with him. He grabbed two cinnamon twists from the next bin, and two chocolate-glazed devil's food doughnuts from the bottom bin. After checking to make sure the sisters were not around, he slipped out of the bakery and into the refectory. This was the part of Gus's being back that stressed him the most. Tucking the sack beneath his blazer, he headed into the main hall and toward the back door. He was about to leave the building when he heard someone behind him. He stopped and turned back.

"Master MacCready," Abbot Ambrose said, looking over the top of his half-moon spectacles. "I'd like a word with you."

"Yes, Abbot Ambrose," Charlie said and glanced to his right and left for a place to stash his bag.

"You can bring that sack of pastries with you," Abbot

Ambrose said. He turned around and led Charlie down the main hall to his office.

"You may put the bag on my desk and have a seat," Abbot Ambrose said, and motioned to the empty chair to the left of the large oak desk.

"Yes, Father Abbot."

Charlie set the paper sack down and sat in the chair nearest the door.

"I suppose you've heard that Master Kugele ran away from the orphanage a month ago?"

"Really?" Charlie said, pretending to be surprised, but the look on the abbot's face told him he was not convincing. "Yes, Abbot Ambrose."

"Have you seen him?"

Charlie looked at the floor.

"I'll take that as a yes," Abbot Ambrose said. "I'll cut to the chase. I know you, Master Miller, and Master Walters have been hiding him in the orchard cabin."

Charlie's head raised sharply and his mouth gaped in surprise. "How did you find out?"

Abbot Ambrose's head tilted to the right. "Son, by now you should know that nothing that goes on on this hilltop happens without my knowledge."

"Oh, please, don't send him back."

"You know he can't stay there."

"I know, but you can't send him back. That place is awful. He'll die there."

"That's a bit of an exaggeration, wouldn't you say?" Abbot Ambrose said. The corners of his mouth curled into a smile beneath his long white beard and mustache.

"He hates it there," Charlie said.

"I know," Abbot Ambrose said.

"Please, can't he stay here?"

"That is not up to me."

"Well, who then?"

"He's still a ward of the state. They will have the final

say in the matter."

"But what if he wanted to stay here? What if he said he wanted to be a monk or a priest or something?"

"Or something?" Again, Abbot Ambrose had to stop himself from laughing out loud. "Son, we both know Master Kugele does not want to pursue a religious life."

"He doesn't know what he wants to do," Charlie said. "He's like all of us. None of us are sure about our futures. One thing is for certain, he doesn't want to go back there."

"I know." Abbot Ambrose nodded. "I tell you what, take your bag of doughnuts to him. Convince him to come back here so I may have a talk with him. We'll see where it goes from there."

Charlie stood up cautiously. He took the paper sack. "Okay. I'll talk to him. Thank you, Abbot Ambrose."

"I can't promise anything, but it's the only way," Abbot Ambrose said. "Tell Master Miller and Master Walters to help you if you need it."

"I will."

Charlie slipped back into the hallway. He felt like a total loser. Gus had been hiding in the cabin for only a week, and already the cat was out of the bag. He headed down the front steps and for the cabin.

The road seemed longer, or else Charlie was taking slower and smaller steps. He dreaded telling Gus that Abbot Ambrose knew about him, but he knew he had to figure out some way of easing the blow. He knocked on the door, two short knocks and then a single knock. He listened for the board that locked the door to be removed. The door finally opened, and to Charlie's surprise, both Howard and Rick were still waiting inside with Gus.

"It's about time," Rick said. "He's nearly finished with the milk I smuggled out of the refectory."

"Here's your breakfast," Charlie said, setting the bag down on the table.

"Gee, thanks," Gus said, grabbing a chocolate doughnut

and putting half of it into his mouth.

"Hey, slow down there. You'll choke," Rick warned and slid the small glass milk bottle across the table toward Gus.

"What took you so long?" Howard asked.

"I got caught," Charlie said, looking straight at Gus, who was already starting on his second pastry. "Abbot Ambrose stopped me as I was about to go out the back door."

"What did you tell him?" Howard asked.

"Nothing."

"You mean, he just let you go?"

"Not exactly," Charlie said. "He already knows about Gus."

Gus choked. Rick vigorously patted Gus's back with one hand and handed him the bottle of milk with his other. Gus took a drink wash down his donut. "You told him?" he asked.

"No, Gus. He already knew you were here."

Gus began to fidget and look around as if preparing to run.

"But it's okay," Charlie said, trying to calm him.

"Okay? He's gonna send me back."

"No, no. I told him you can't go back there. He just wants to talk to you. That's all."

Gus shook his head. "No, no. It's a trap. I go up there and he'll have those spawn of Satan waiting for me. I'm outta here."

"Gus, please, give him a chance," Charlie pleaded.

"I'm with Gus," Rick said. "You should have lied."

"Like I'm any good at that?" Charlie said and glared at Rick. "Besides, if anyone can make it so Gus can stay here, it's Abbot Ambrose. Gus, please. Worse case is they send you back and you run away again."

"That's your idea of an option?" Howard said. "Boy, you're as good at plan making as you are at lying—not at all."

"You're not helping, Howard. Gus, please. I promise, if he tries to send you away, I'll go with you."

"He's not going to send you away. You've said it

yourself, you're not an orphan like me."

"Do you see my parents anywhere? No. So, I might as well be."

Gus was taken aback by Charlie's tone as much as by what he said. He glanced at Rick and then Howard before looking back at Charlie. "Okay. I'll talk to him. But let me finish eating first."

Charlie laughed, feeling relieved and sat down. "Sure thing, buddy. Take your time."

"It will be like eating my last meal before my execution," Gus said, taking a fritter from the bag. "Glad I saved this one 'til last."

"It won't be that bad," Charlie said, though he was not so sure.

Charlie waited quietly while Gus finished eating. When he was through, he wadded up the paper bag and threw it at the fireplace. It missed and landed on the floor instead.

"I guess I won't be going out for basketball," he said. He sounded defeated. "Well, let's get it over with."

"Gus, I'm really sorry. I didn't tell him, honest," Charlie said.

"That's okay. I knew I would be found out eventually."

"Yeah, but I didn't think it would be this fast," Rick said with all the venom he could muster, and glared at Charlie.

"Better be careful you don't choke on your spit," Charlie said to Rick and followed the others out the door.

Gus and Rick walked side by side ahead of Howard and Charlie.

"Honestly, I don't know how Abbot Ambrose found out," Charlie said. "I know Gus and Rick blame me, but I didn't say a word."

"I know you didn't," Howard said. "Because I did."

"You did?" Charlie said, almost raising his voice enough for Gus and Rick to hear.

"Keep it down," Howard warned. "Yes, I told him. I had to. Gus can't live out here forever. He needs to be in school. He needs to graduate so whatever he decides to do with his life, he'll have a fighting chance."

"Do you think he'll let Gus stay?"

"I don't know," Howard answered. "I did my best to make it happen, but who listens to a kid? That's how they all view us, as kids. They don't seem to get it, that we're almost adults. Did you know that the term Master, the way they use it, refers to a boy? Mister is what men are called."

"I never thought of it like that," Charlie said.

"Well, I'm tired of it."

"What can you do about it? You can't change the way they do things. We're guests in their world. Long after we're gone, they will still be here. Don't make our last year together more stressful than it already is," Charlie said.

"Honestly, you need a backbone, Charlie," Howard said. "You need some fight in you. Like when you think of your parents and how they let you down."

Charlie listened. Deep down, he understood what Howard was saying. Still, he was at a loss as to what they could do about their current problem.

When they reached the Abbot's office door, the three gave Gus a hug and told him they would wait for him. He thanked them, and then knocked on the door.

"*Ave*," Father Abbott called out from inside.

Gus nervously opened the door. Glancing one last time at them, he said, "Wait here." And then he was gone.

"I can't believe this," Rick said. His arms were folded over his thin, bony chest and his teeth were clenched. He paced back and forth in front of the Abbot's door. "He's going to send Gus away and it's all your fault, MacCready."

"Oh, shut up, Walters. You don't know shit."

"Howard!" Charlie said sharply.

"Well, he doesn't." Howard said, and sat down in one of the two wooden chairs across the hall by Father Mark's office door. Charlie took the seat beside him.

"This is not fair. He shouldn't be forced to go back to

that place," Rick continued his tirade.

"Rick, we don't know what Abbot Ambrose will do," Charlie said. "He may surprise you and find a way for Gus to stay."

"And pigs may sprout wings and fly. Wake up, Pollyanna."

"I think I know my great-uncle a little better than you," Charlie said.

"What?" Rick gasped. He stopped pacing and looked back and forth between the two of them.

"Yes, Abbot Ambrose is my great-uncle, my grandmother's brother."

Slowly Rick's mouth opened wider. He glanced at the office door and then at Charlie. "It's all making sense. That's why you're the abbot's pet. It's nepotism."

"What are you talking about?" Howard said.

"That's why Charlie got to be in the Altar Boys Club his first year here," Rick said.

"You don't know what you're talking about," Howard said. He leaned closer to Charlie. "What's nepotism?" he whispered.

"I don't know. I'll look it up later," Charlie whispered back.

Rick began pacing again and shaking his head. "I knew I should never have trusted you. Ha! That's why you got away with going up to the attic and the bell tower without getting in trouble."

"That would be my doing," Howard said.

Rick stopped again. "What? Is he your uncle too?"

"God, Walters, you can be pretty stupid sometimes," Howard said. "No, he's not my uncle."

"Then why do you get special treatment?"

"Because I'm not a jackass."

"Howard!"

"It's okay, it's in the Bible. I'll show you," Howard said, to calm Charlie.

"Still, Abbot Ambrose has ears. He can hear you."

"As can I," Father Mark said, standing in the doorway to his office with his arms folded over his chest. "I suggest you take this outside unless all three of you want to spend your weekend with work crew."

"We're waiting for Gus," Rick said.

"Master Kugele?" Father Mark asked, glancing at the Abbot's office door. "Then keep it down and no more foul language, Master Miller."

"Yes, Father," Howard said.

They waited until Father Mark retreated back into his office and closed the door.

Howard leaned closer to Charlie. "That was a close one," he said, and cringed.

Rick paced away the minutes and hours while Charlie kept shifting around in his chair. Father Mark's office door opened, and he entered the hallway. He looked at the boys.

"Still waiting?" he said. "It's about time for lunch. You boys had better go."

"But—"

"Master Kugele will still be here when you are through," he said, looking at Howard.

"Yes, Father."

The dean walked across the hall and disappeared into Abbot Ambrose's office.

Charlie stood up and stretched. He rubbed his bum and looked at the wooden chair. "Too bad those chairs don't have a cushion."

"They aren't meant to be comfortable," Rick said. "They are meant to be torture."

"Well, they succeeded," Howard said.

"What do you think Father Mark meant by Gus will still be here after lunch?" Rick asked.

"Probably that he will be here when we finish eating?" Howard said with as much sarcasm as he could muster.

Charlie tilted his head to the side and let out a sigh. "He

probably means they are still figuring out what to do with Gus."

"I hope it's good news," Rick said.

Charlie found lunch hard to eat. Not because the food was bad; he was just too worried about Gus. Even though Howard said he told the Abbot about Gus, Charlie still felt guilty because he was caught and had to turn Gus in. It felt like a betrayal.

After the boys were dismissed, Charlie returned to the main hallway and his waiting chair. It was not long before Howard and Rick joined him.

"Did you remember to make a sandwich for Gus?" Charlie asked as Howard sat down in the chair beside him.

"Of course," Howard answered and pulled a flattened sandwich wrapped in a white paper napkin from the pocket of his blazer. Charlie frowned.

"Could you hear if they are still in there?" Rick asked Charlie.

"Yes. I heard Father Mark's voice when I sat down."

"What did he say?"

"I couldn't make it out."

"Well, at least they are still talking."

"What did you expect, Walters? That they would be sitting in there staring at each other? Of course, they're talking."

"Come on, Howard, be nice. We're all worried," Charlie said.

"Yeah, well...."

The sound of the door to the student wing opening startled the boys. With wide eyes, they watched as two nuns entered. Neither spoke to the boys. They walked directly to the Abbot's door and knocked. The door opened and they entered.

"Oh no," Rick said. "That doesn't look good."

"Did you see the expression on their faces?" Howard said. "It looked like they sucked on a lemon all the way here."

Charlie chuckled quietly to himself. He did not dare risk commenting for fear he would laugh out loud.

"Do you think they will force Gus to go back?"

"How should I know?" Howard answered Rick. "We just have to wait and see."

"Well, I'm tired of waiting."

"No one is keeping you here. You're free to go whenever it is you want."

Rick stopped pacing and glared at Howard. "Just for that, I'm staying."

"Shoot yourself."

"It's suit yourself," Rick corrected.

"I know what I said," Howard answered back.

Charlie put his head back against the wall and closed his eyes. He did not intend on falling asleep. It was just that watching Rick's constant pacing was making him feel a bit nauseous. Sleep happened though. The next thing he knew, Howard was nudging him awake.

"What?" Charlie asked in a groggy voice.

"It's nearly three o'clock, and they're still at it."

"What happened to Rick?"

"He went to the restroom."

"Oh. Are the nuns still in there?"

"No, they left a little while ago. They didn't look too happy either."

"I wonder what that means?"

"I think it's a good sign."

"I hope so."

The office door opened and Father Mark walked into the hall. He looked at the two. "Still here?"

"Yes, Father," they answered together.

Gus entered the hallway followed closely by Abbot Ambrose.

"Does this mean what I think it does?" Charlie asked.

"It will take a lot more discussion before a final decision is made, but for now, Master Kugele is going to be staying with us, and attending classes beginning Monday," Abbot Ambrose said.

"All right!" Howard shouted and jumped to his feet.

Charlie could not help being swept up in the excitement. "I knew you wouldn't let us down."

"Don't get your hopes up, boys," Abbot Ambrose said. "This is only temporary. For now, I understand there is an empty bed in Saint Nicholas dorm."

"Yes. It's in Gus's old cubicle," Charlie said, then looked at Gus. "You'll be sharing it with a guy named Robin but you'll like him. He's a good guy."

Gus still had not shown any hint of excitement. In fact, he had not said a word. Instead, he looked worried.

"Can we go, now?" Charlie asked.

"Yes, you may go. Father Mark will make sure you have a uniform, Master Kugele and the rest of your things from the orphanage are being sent."

"Yes, Father Abbot. Thank you," he said. "Thank you, too, Father Mark. I'm sorry for all the trouble I've caused. Really."

"Well, what's done is done. We just need to figure out how to fix things. Run along now," Abbot Ambrose said, in his usual gentle tone.

The boys waited until they reached the stairs before they spoke.

"So, what happened in there?" Howard asked.

"I'm tired. I'll tell you later," Gus answered.

They were about to head up the stairs when Rick came out of the restroom. He caught sight of Gus and rushed across the hallway.

"What's going on?" he asked.

"We're taking Gus up to Saint Nicholas dorm," Charlie reported.

Rick's eyes widened and he grinned. "Does this mean he gets to stay?"

"For now," Gus said. He turned around and started up the stairs. "I know the way," he said and left the three behind.

Charlie caught up with Gus when he was about to enter their dorm.

"Gus," he called to him.

Gus stopped and let go of the door.

"Is everything okay?" Charlie asked.

"Yes." His answer was quick and clipped.

Charlie studied Gus's expression. He looked tired. Thinking it best not to question him further, he grabbed the door handle and pulled the door open. "Come on, I'll introduce you to Robin."

After getting Gus settled, Charlie went to find Howard. He caught up with him in Saint Thomas.

"How's Gus?" Howard asked, putting his comic book down beside him and sitting up on the edge of his bed.

"He's napping before dinner. I warned the other guys not to wake him and if they do, they'll each get an hour of work crew."

Howard laughed. "Do you think Brother Simon will back you up?"

"Probably not, but it sure scared the guys," Charlie said.

"You guys talking about Gus?" Rick asked while he approached Howard's cubicle.

"What are you doing in here?" Howard snapped.

"Howard, be nice," Charlie said. "Yes. He's napping right now."

"Did he say what is happening?"

"No."

"Can't you ask your uncle to let him stay?"

"First of all, he's my great-uncle, and secondly, I already have but he said it is out of his hands. Gus is still a ward of the state and therefore, it's up to them," Charlie said.

"Well, it seems if Abbot Ambrose were to ask, whoever in the state office would approve it."

"You'd think that, wouldn't you, Walters," Howard said. "But it doesn't work like that. You've heard of separation of church and state?"

"Oh, that's different."

"Not really," Howard said, sounding bored with Rick.

"Well, whatever the case, we just have to be patient. I'm sure Abbot Ambrose will figure something out. At least for now, Gus is staying here," Charlie said.

"True," Rick said. "But it is different, Howie."

"Always have to have the last word, don't you, Walters," Howard said.

"No, I don't."

Howard looked at Charlie and grinned. Charlie held his breath to stifle a laugh.

TRYOUTS

Two weeks had passed since Gus returned. Still, there was no final decision about his being allowed to stay. Charlie asked his great-uncle, but all Abbot Ambrose would say was, "We're working on it." Charlie could not understand why it was so complicated, when in his mind it was an easy decision.

"You're still worried about your friend," Father Cecil said as he rested his hand on Charlie's shoulder while they walked across the Great Lawn.

"Yes," Charlie answered.

"Does Master Kugele want to stay now?"

"I think so. He seems to like that we're all back together again."

"That's great."

"But I have a feeling that something bad is going to happen. That he isn't going to get to stay."

"I understand your fears, but try not to worry so much about what might happen that you don't enjoy the time you all have together."

"I'll try," Charlie said.

"So, have you thought anymore about what you want to do after graduation?"

"Howard thinks we should take a road trip and find my parents."

"Does he, now? Interesting," Father Cecil said. "What do you think about that?"

"I told him it would be a waste of time. I don't want to look for them. They haven't bothered to look for me all these years."

"I see. What would you like to do?"

"I don't know yet. I just—it's a huge decision."

"That's true."

"Did you know that Brother Linus used to act on Broadway?"

"Yes," Father Cecil said with a nod and a smile. He heard Charlie's enthusiasm rise. "He was in several musicals, *Hair* and *Cabaret.* He played one of the apostles in *Godspell.*"

"Really? He didn't mention that one."

"No, I don't imagine he would. He's a humble man."

"What else did he act in?"

"Oh, he was Snoopy in the production of *You're a Good Man, Charlie Brown.* I imagine that would have been fun to see."

"I'll say. Maybe that's what I'll do. Go see a Broadway play or something after I graduate."

"That sounds more like a vacation than a career."

"True. Figuring out what I want to be is really hard since all I ever wanted was to be part of a family, and now that's never going to happen."

"At least not in the way you imagined. Perhaps you will get married and have a family of your own?"

"Oh, I doubt that," Charlie said. "For some reason I've never pictured myself married and having children."

"How do you see yourself then?"

Charlie thought hard but nothing came to mind. He had put all his hopes and dreams into being a boy with parents that he never imagined his life as a man. "I don't know," he finally answered.

"Well, you have time," Father Cecil said.

"Speaking of time." Charlie glanced at his pocket watch. "We should start back to the Abbey. It's almost time for Vespers."

"Very well, lead the way, dear boy."

By the time they reached the Abbey, Charlie took Father Cecil directly to the church where he joined his brothers in the choir stalls on either side of the chancel. Charlie thought about leaving, but decided to stay and watch. He slipped into the pew by one of the marble pillars in the nave and sat down. As the brothers chanted and prayed, Charlie watched with keen interest. He had participated in Vespers with the brothers on several occasions over the years, but for some reason, this time it seemed different. When it was finished, Charlie made his exit.

When Charlie entered the student wing, he noticed that the boys were already beginning to line up outside the refectory for dinner. Instead of returning to his dorm, he decided to take his place in line. To the boys' dismay, Gus was not assigned to any of their tables. He had been assigned to a table of his own with students he did not know. Charlie wished Gus were at his table. Instead, he was stuck with Robert Muster, two sophomores, and two freshmen whose names he could never seem to remember. They were members of Saint Peter and Saint Thomas dorms, and since they were underclassmen, their paths rarely crossed. Robert knew them, however, and he seemed to keep them in line.

After dessert was finished, Father Mark stood up at the head table. He rattled off the work crew assignments for the boys who had been disciplined and then he picked up a sheet of paper from the table behind him.

"Our last announcement is a fun one," he said, adjusting his gold-rimmed glasses so he could see the printing on the page. "Brother Linus wanted me to announce that he will be directing our first major production in our new gymnasium. Tryouts for Charles Dickens' *A Christmas Carol* will begin next Monday after classes. I'll post a cast list with character descriptions on the bulletin board in the lounge. Tryouts are opened to everyone interested. That is all I have."

The boys bowed their heads and Father Mark concluded the meal with a prayer.

"Did you hear that?" Rick said as the four met in the hall outside the refectory. "*A Christmas Carol*. I'm going to try out for Bob Cratchit."

"Why not go for old Scrooge?" Howard said.

"I figured that was your role."

"Very funny," Howard said with a scowl.

"What about you, Gus?" Rick asked. "I think you would make a great Ghost of Christmas Present."

"I don't know," Gus answered.

"Why not?"

"I may not be here by then."

The excitement and smiles on the boys' faces drained instantly.

"Why? What have you heard?" Rick asked.

"Nothing," Gus answered. "That's the problem."

"Well, you should plan on staying," Rick said.

"Why? So, when I'm sent away, I can be really depressed? Thanks, but no thanks. I'm going to do what Abbot Ambrose said, plan for the worst and hope for the best."

"That's what I'm saying," Rick said.

Gus shook his head. "We'll see."

Charlie could tell by Gus's tone that he was slipping into a depression already. "Let's forget about the play. Let's go do something fun. It's Friday night. What's on TV?"

~§~

The weekend flew by for Charlie. He received a letter from his grandmother on Saturday. She was a bit saddened because one of the ladies she dined with had moved to a new senior living home. Other than that, it was the usual don't tell anyone about the key, the box, and the letter. Reading the warning again, Charlie felt a twinge of guilt that he had already told Howard, but Howard was good at keeping his secrets.

Monday morning, sitting in a darkened classroom, watching a film on television commercials and truth in advertising, Charlie's thoughts drifted between feeling guilty about telling Howard about the box and wondering if what the film was talking about was really a problem. He could not figure out the point Father Vicar was trying to make. After all, Father Vicar did not do the shopping for the abbey. Still, it was Modern Problems class. Charlie guessed false ads could be considered a problem. He yawned in the dark.

Halfway through the movie, the door opened and the light from the hall momentarily washed out the picture on the screen. Everyone looked at the visitor, who walked directly to Father Vicar at the projector. He whispered something before collecting Gus and leaving the room. Charlie turned around to look at Howard.

"Master MacCready, the screen is in the front of the class. Turn around," Father Vicar said.

Charlie did as he was told but his mind was now off and running.

After class, Rick approached the two.

"Who was that? Why did he want Gus?" he asked.

"It was Brother Conrad," Howard answered. "And why do you think he took Gus? The abbot must have an answer about Gus staying here."

"Well, he can't make him leave now," Rick said.

"Wanna bet? He can do whatever he wants and whenever."

Charlie noticed the disdain in Howard's tone. He felt sorry for his great-uncle. The decision on whether Gus stayed or left, Charlie understood, was not up to the abbot. It was up to the state, whoever that was, and yet, Abbot Ambrose would get the blame.

"Boys, shouldn't you be heading to your next class?" Brother Linus said as he stood by the door.

"Yes, Brother," they answered, and grabbed their books.

Charlie was distracted all through choir practice. His mind was on Gus while he sang on autopilot. Even when the choirmaster, Father Aloysius, hushed everyone so he could chastise one of the boys in the front, Charlie was not listening.

Finally, the bell rang and everyone headed back to their homerooms to stow their songbooks and call it a day. Charlie, Howard, and Rick headed down to the first floor. Howard put his ear close to the abbot's door. He listened for a while and then turned back to the other two.

"Nothing. I don't think he's in there."

"I didn't hear anything in Father Mark's office either." Rick reported.

"I wonder where they could be?" Charlie said.

"Let's go check the dorm," Rick suggested.

"You go ahead. I'm gonna take a look outside."

"I'll go with you," Howard said to Charlie.

"Fine, if he's upstairs, I won't be coming down to find you."

"That's okay with us," Howard said.

Rick hurried away while Charlie and Howard went in the opposite direction.

"Hey, don't get down," Howard said consolingly. "We don't know what they decided to do. He could still be staying."

"I know," Charlie said, feeling deep inside as though he were falling down a dark hole. "It's just if he were staying, where is he? Where're Father Mark, Abbot Ambrose? Wouldn't they be in their offices or celebrating?"

"Just because they aren't in their offices doesn't mean anything. They do have other stuff to do. Besides, aren't tryouts this afternoon?"

"Yes," Charlie said.

"Well, let's go watch the guys make fools of themselves. It's obvious we won't find out anything here," Howard said, looking down the empty front steps of the abbey.

"Okay," Charlie said. His mood lifted a bit.

The boys ran across the Great Lawn to the gymnasium where Brother Linus was holding the tryouts. They walked through the main doors and were immediately struck by the sound of chatter. There were already a bunch of college students gathered as well as a few from the high school. They were seated in chairs that were set up in neat rows in front of the stage. Brother Linus and his two assistants, whom Charlie did not recognize, were standing in front of the stage on the main floor. They had clipboards and papers. While Brother Linus talked to them, one appeared to be taking notes.

"Let's sit over here," Howard said, ushering Charlie to the empty chairs in the back row, center.

They sat and ducked down, not wanting to be included in the casting call.

"Wonder when they're going to start?" Howard asked.

"Dunno," Charlie answered.

"There you are," Rick whispered loudly and sat down beside Charlie. "Why didn't you remind me about tryouts? I was heading upstairs when I overheard a group of guys talking about it. I could have missed it."

"Sorry, I forgot about it, too," Charlie said.

Brother Linus silenced everyone with the ding from a bell. "We're going to begin by casting the main characters in the play first," he said to the group of twenty-some students. "I'd like those trying out for the role of Scrooge to stand."

Charlie watched as two college students and one of the monks stood up. "I didn't know monks were allowed to act in plays," he whispered to Howard.

"Why not? Brother Linus is the director and he's a monk."

"Yeah, but that's different." Charlie settled back in his chair.

The three candidates huddled around one of the assistants who handed each a slip of paper.

Next Brother Linus called for those trying out for Bob

Cratchit. Howard nudged Charlie with his elbow and laughed when they saw Rick stand up.

"This should be good. He doesn't stand a chance," Howard said when he saw the group of five guys head toward the other assistant.

"Just because the others are in college doesn't mean anything," Charlie said, but he had to admit, it did not look good for Rick.

"Then I want to have those trying out for the four ghosts—Marley, Christmas Past, Present, and Future—to get ready."

Another large group stood up and moved to the side. The first assistant took everyone backstage. The lights in the gym dimmed and the stage curtain opened. A desk lamp turned on, illuminating a small table in front of Brother Linus and his second assistant. They were seated in the center of the rows of chairs, about four rows in front of Charlie.

"Okay, I'm ready for the first group," Brother Linus called out.

One by one the Scrooge-wannabes stepped forward and read their lines. During each performance, Brother Linus scribbled some notes down on his pad of paper. After the three were finished, he asked them all to stay while he auditioned the Cratchit group. There were more notes and some cringes but when they were all finished, Brother Linus asked for only two to remain. To both Howard's and Charlie's surprise, Rick was one of the two.

Brother Linus then called one of the Scrooges forward and had him read lines with each Cratchit. He did this with each Scrooge.

Casting the first two ghosts, Marley and Christmas Past, went fast. There were only two trying out for each role.

"This is the part I want to see," Howard whispered. "The movie version had a great Christmas Present."

When Brother Linus called those trying out for Christmas Present to all walk onto the stage, Charlie and

Howard sat straight up in their seats. Gus was among the group of four guys.

"What?" Howard whispered.

Charlie looked at Rick who was standing beside the Scrooge-wannabes and other Cratchits. Rick's mouth was gaping and his eyes were bulging wide. Charlie knew Rick had seen Gus, too.

Brother Linus gave his instructions to them all and then one by one they ran through their lines. To Charlie's amazement, Gus was really good. He was not as large as one of the guys trying out, but his voice carried, and sounded jolly.

"I hope he gets the part," Charlie whispered to Howard.

When they were finished, the first assistant walked onto the stage. "That's all of them," she announced.

"What do you mean? No one's trying out for Christmas Future?"

The assistant shook her head. She then held up her hand to shade her eyes while she looked out at the audience. Charlie cringed and sank a bit lower in his seat. Brother Linus turned around and noticed the two of them.

"All right," he said. "You two get up on stage."

"But we're not trying out," Howard protested.

"Well, you are now. Get up there, or you will have work crew for the rest of the year."

Charlie and Howard looked at each other. They stood up and moved to the aisle.

"Can he really do that?" Howard whispered.

"I don't know, but I don't want to find out either," Charlie answered.

Once they were center stage, Brother Linus asked all the others still standing to come back down and take a seat behind him. With the stage cleared except for the two boys, Brother Linus began his instructions.

"Now, I know the two of you have been to a funeral," he said. "What I want you to do—can I get two chairs on stage," he called to his assistant. She immediately brough two folding chairs from backstage. "Place them just left of center stage, facing each other, perfect," he instructed. "Now, what I would like you each to do, one at a time, is walk up to the chairs as if they were a casket. Look at your friend, shake your head slowly, turn and walk back to where you started. Can you do that?"

"Sure," Howard said.

"Fine, Howard, you will go first," Brother Linus said.

Charlie was caught off guard by Brother Linus calling Howard by his first name and not Master Miller. It took him a while to refocus his thoughts and watch his friend's audition. Howard started out strutting.

"Stop!" Brother Linus shouted. "Not so cocky. Walk up like you don't really want to but you have to. Now try it again. Remember, this is your friend."

Howard started over and again Brother Linus stopped him. "Pretend you are an old man."

After Howard's fourth attempt, good or bad, it was Charlie's turn. He was so nervous his hands trembled as he walked across the stage toward the chairs. Once he reached the pretend coffin, his feet became planted, he could not move. Slowly he shook his head and turned away, willing his feet to move. He made it back to Howard's side with much effort and no interruption.

"Good job," Howard said.

"I don't remember a scene like that in the movie," Charlie said.

"Neither do I. Oh well," Howard answered, with a shrug of his shoulders.

"That will be all for today," Brother Linus said. "Once casting is finished for the other characters, we'll post the decision on the bulletin board inside the gym door here. Yes, Rick."

"When would that be?" Rick asked.

"We should have the casting done by this Friday and the results posted Saturday. That will be all."

There was a rumbling as the remaining hopefuls

gathered their things and left the gymnasium. Charlie and Howard met Rick outside and waited for Gus to emerge. When he did, they rushed him.

"Where have you been?" Rick asked.

"I thought you said you weren't going to try out for the play because you didn't know if you were staying?" Howard said.

"That's right, I did," Gus said.

"So, does this mean you are staying?" Charlie asked with a bit of trepidation.

Gus looked at their faces and slowly began to grin. "Yes. Abbot Ambrose gave me the decision when he took me out of class."

"So, what dorm are you in?" Howard asked.

Gus looked at each of them. It was easy when they were all in the same dorm, but now they were in three separate dorms. "I've been assigned to Saint Nicholas," he answered.

"No way," Rick said. "Why didn't you ask to be in Saint Peter?"

Gus looked at Rick. "Are you forgetting I already tried that?"

"Don't be silly, that was a long time ago and Dougary and his goons are gone."

"I know that. I just wanted to be in my old cubicle," Gus said.

"But you have to share it with Robin Muster," Rick said. "And he's a junior."

"I know. That's okay."

"So, where did you disappear to? I mean, why didn't you come back to class?" Howard asked.

"Father Mark took me to town to buy a few things I need, some new clothes and stuff. We made it back right when Brother Linus called for the ghosts."

"That is wonderful," Charlie said and gave his buddy a hug. Howard took a turn next and then Rick did as well.

"By the way," Charlie said. "Your audition was the

best."

"Yours wasn't so bad either," Gus said and then looked at Howard. "Sorry."

"Hey, that's fine with me. I was trying to throw it."

"You were?" Charlie said.

"Yep."

"I thought you were really going for it."

"No way. You did great, though."

"I was petrified. My hands were shaking and then my feet felt like lead weights. I couldn't move."

"Well, that must have been what Brother Linus was looking for because he didn't ask you to do it over."

"What about me?" Rick asked. "How did I look up there?"

"Meh," Howard said. "I've seen better."

"Don't listen to him, you did great. I wouldn't be surprised if you get the part."

"Thanks, Charlie," Rick said with a grin but then glared at Howard. "Eat rocks, Miller."

"Eat rocks," Howard repeated and laughed. "Where did you hear that?"

"I don't swear like you. Think about it," Rick said.

Howard cocked his head to the side for a moment and then a look of realization came over him. "Hey, back at you!" he said.

The rest of the week passed quickly. Gus was settled in, and Charlie felt as if a weight had been lifted. He wanted to thank Abbot Ambrose, but Father Mark said the abbot had been called away and would not be back for several weeks. Charlie wondered what that meant and where his great-uncle had gone.

When Saturday came, Charlie had forgotten all about his impromptu tryout. It was not until Rick told him at lunch that he got the part of Christmas Future that he remembered. Still, he did not trust Rick, and thought he was pulling his leg. After lunch he grabbed Howard and the two rushed to the gym.

Sure enough, tacked on the bulletin board and in black,

typed print was the cast sheet. Charlie quickly scanned the page. He looked at the role of Bob Cratchit first and saw Rick's name. Next, Christmas Present. To his delight, Gus had won the role.

"Oh no!" Howard said.

Charlie looked below at Christmas Future and saw his name. He felt horrified at first, then excited at being chosen, and then horrified all over again.

"Now what?" Howard said.

"I can't do it."

"You have to. You were perfect. Besides, there was no one else and I sure as hell am not doing it."

"Howard! Language."

"Well, I'm not."

"I need to talk to Father Cecil," Charlie said and pushed the gym door open.

Moments later, Charlie was sitting on the concrete bench beside Father Cecil and staring at the goldfish in the pond.

"That is wonderful," the monk said, grinning proudly.

"No, it's not. I can't do it," Charlie said, desperate for someone to agree with him.

"Why? What prevents you from participating in the play?"

"When I auditioned, I was shaking like a leaf and I could barely walk."

"You'll get over that."

"But what if I trip? What if I say the wrong thing?"

"First of all, as I recall, the Ghost of Christmas Future doesn't speak. So, you don't have to say anything. Secondly, why so negative? What if you do it and have a lot of fun? Son, do you recall the first time you served at Mass? Were you nervous?"

"I think so. I don't remember."

"Exactly. Are you nervous now when you serve at Mass?"

"No."

"My point exactly," Father Cecil said and patted

Charlie's knee. "Before you walk out on stage in front of an audience, you will have weeks of practicing. Brother Linus will help you get over your nervousness."

"But—"

Father Cecil put up his hand. "Instead of looking for all the reasons to not do the play, look for reasons to do it. Think of the joy the play will bring to someone in the audience. Perhaps seeing it will be the only Christmas gift they receive this year.

"Son, I heard in your voice how excited you were to show me the stage and everything behind it. I'm blind and couldn't see but your enthusiasm and descriptions helped to visualize what you were looking at. This will be good for you. Relax and enjoy the ride."

Charlie thought about what his friend said. "Okay," he said. "I'll do it."

"That's my good boy. I knew you would understand. You'll do great."

After returning Father Cecil to his room, Charlie picked up his script from Brother Linus and thanked him for selecting him for the role.

"We will have our first read through Monday afternoon," he told Charlie. "I know you don't have any lines, but you need to be there to start hearing your cues."

"I'll be there," Charlie assured the director.

AUTUMN

As the weeks passed, the days grew colder. Fall had arrived with a vengeance and showed no signs of mercy. It stripped the dogwood trees on the Great Lawn of their leaves and sent the goldfish to the bottom of the ponds. They only swam to the surface when there was food. While Charlie led Father Cecil across the Great Lawn to their favorite pond, he felt a chill. He envied Father Cecil's heavy wool cape.

"How are your classes going?" the blind monk asked.

"Fine. I received my grades for the first term. I got a C in Father Vicar's class. I should have gotten a B at least, according to my grades on the tests. I think it's because he hates me."

Father Cecil chuckled quietly. "Hate is a strong word."

"But it's true. He does hate me. I heard the way he talked about me to Abbot Ambrose and the archbishop."

"I'm sure he may come across that way. Vicar does need a lesson in tactfulness."

"It's so unfair," Charlie said, thinking about his average grade. "I really worked hard for that class."

"Well, don't worry too much about it. Just stay focused

on the next term. You'll do fine," Father Cecil said and squeezed Charlie's shoulder. "What about rehearsals? How are they coming along?"

"Oh, I wish you could see," Charlie said. "The people who are building the sets are incredible. I've never seen anything like it before. Part of the stage is on this huge turntable-like platform that turns all the way around. It's divided in half. One side is a wall with a fireplace inside of Scrooge's house, the other is the street outside his house. Oh, and then beside it is a wall that breaks away to show a cemetery. That's for my part."

Father Cecil smiled as he listened to the excitement in Charlie's voice. Never before had he wanted to see as much as he did at that moment. "It sounds wonderful."

"Oh, it's more than wonderful. It's magical," Charlie said.

"How are you doing with your scenes?"

"Fine," Charlie said confidently. "The lights are all out when it's my turn to go on stage. I have to follow a path of glow in the dark dots on the floor to find Scrooge's bed. Then I pull back the curtains on his four-poster bed and look at him as the lights come on. He says his first line and I nod, once. He says another line and I nod again. Then he says a third line and I slowly shake my head no while I turn around and walk slowly across the stage. That's when the stage turns around to show the street scene. After that, I turn the other way and point at the wall as it splits in two. Scrooge screams and the lights go out. I follow the glow in the dark dots off stage. That's it."

"Sounds like you have it down."

"Yes, I think so."

"So, are you still nervous?"

"Not really. Well, maybe a little."

"By opening night you'll be fine," Father Cecil assured him. "Tell me, how is your friend Master Kugele doing?"

"He's doing really well. He likes it here. I think being in that orphanage was harder than he imagined it would be, and he realized that living here was better."

"Well, I'm happy he's happy. Have you given any more thought to what you want to do after graduation? It's only six months away."

"No," Charlie answered with a sigh in his voice. "Howard is still intent on the road trip. I keep telling him I don't want to. In fact, if my parents showed up here today, I'm not sure I would want to see them."

"Surely you don't mean that," Father Cecil said.

"Why not? In fifteen years, they couldn't even take a small risk and call me or my grandma, send a card through a friend or something. No, I don't want anything to do with them. My childhood is over, as everyone keeps reminding me. I don't need them anymore."

Father Cecil did not speak. He sat quietly beside his young friend on the bench while he processed what he heard. "What are your plans for Thanksgiving?" he asked, changing the subject.

"Plans? Nothing." Charlie answered. "Howard invited me to go to his dad's but now that Gus is here, I don't want to leave him behind."

"That's very thoughtful of you."

"Besides, after Thanksgiving, things are going to get crazy with the choir's Christmas concerts and the play and classes. I don't know how I'm going to be able to do it all."

"Oh, don't you worry about that," Father Cecil said. "I'm sure you'll manage just fine."

"Father Aloysius booked a concert at The Towers for the choir the first weekend after Thanksgiving break. We have only two practices that week."

"He wouldn't have booked it if he didn't think you were ready. Besides, the concert is always a treat for the elderly residents. They will love it no matter what."

"I suppose," Charlie answered, but he was not as confident as Father Cecil. "The following weekend is the play. We have five shows. The first one is Friday night and then there are two shows on Saturday and two on Sunday. The last show is a special one for the parents."

"That's wonderful."

"Then the following Tuesday, the choir sings with several other choirs from all over the diocese for the archbishop."

"Oh, that should be interesting. Where will it be?"

"I don't know exactly. Some place in Portland, I think. We have to get there early and have a quick rehearsal with the others before we perform for the archbishop."

"Sounds like fun."

"I don't know," Charlie said, already feeling stressed just thinking about everything. "Our final concert is for the parents on the day the student boys go home for Christmas break. I think that will be my least favorite."

"Why is that?"

"Because, Howard will be going home to his dad's. It'll be just the seven of us guys here."

"I'm sure it will still be a blessed holiday. Don't fret too much."

After returning Father Cecil to his room, Charlie headed back to his dorm. There was still an hour before he had to be at his duties in refectory. As he passed by the front desk on the first floor of the abbey wing, he was surprised by a familiar face.

"Hi, Dougary—I mean, Brother Jonah," Charlie greeted.

"Hi," Dougary answered with a smile. "I'm still Dougary. I won't be officially Jonah until Christmas eve when I enter the novitiate. I'm still a postulant."

"Why do they have you manning the front desk?"

"Brother Gregory had to step away for a second," he answered and glanced at the clock on the wall above the foyer door. "But it's been an hour so far. If he doesn't come back soon, Brother Norman will be coming on duty and he won't be pleased."

"Why?"

"Because Brother Norman is in charge of the front desk

and he won't like it that a postulant was left on his own here. Not to mention, postulants are not supposed to talk to anyone other than the brothers."

"Really?" Charlie said.

"Actually, I haven't seen it officially in writing," Dougary said, leaning over the reception counter a little more. "Our novice master says we're to strip off our old personality, whatever that is, and be completely immersed in monastic life. That way we can decide at the end of our postulant year if this is the life we have been called to."

"Year?" Charlie said, confused. "You've only been a postulant for six months."

"For those who have been members of the school, such as myself, the abbot has shortened our postulancy. He said we already have a general idea of what life is like here at the abbey."

"Oh, that makes sense."

Dougary looked over his shoulder toward the hallway. "Where is he?"

"Who? The abbot?"

"No, Brother Gregory," Dougary said. "But, why did you say the abbot?"

"It's just you were talking about the abbot and I was told he was away for several weeks, but that was two months ago. I'm starting to get a little worried that something has happened to him."

"Oh, don't worry about him. He's probably gone to the priory." Dougary looked at the clock on the wall above the door to the foyer. "I'm doomed. Brother Norman will be here any second. He's never late. You better go."

"Okay, sure," Charlie said and hesitantly backed away from the counter and toward the door. "I'll see you later?"

"Sure. Now, go," Dougary urged.

The hallway of the student wing was quiet except for the sound of Charlie's footsteps. When he reached the mail slots, he stopped to look. There was a letter in his pigeonhole.

He took it out and read the return address. It was from his grandmother. Judging from the size and weight, it was a card. She always remembered to send him a card for every holiday. It did not matter if it was one of the big holidays or just a small one like Saint Patrick's Day. She sent a card for them all, sometimes with a little spending money. Charlie carefully tore the end off of the envelope and withdrew the card. It was a cutout card on top with a squared off bottom. The top was cut along the edges of a cartoon turkey's tail feathers. The sight brought a smile to Charlie's lips. He opened the card and a twenty-dollar bill slipped out and fell to the floor. Charlie retrieved it and shoved it into his pocket before returning to the writing inside. It was the usual well wishes for a happy Thanksgiving. Even the handwritten note his grandmother included was not new but very welcome. He closed the card and stuffed it back into the envelope.

He turned toward the stairs and was about to leave when he heard someone singing. It was coming from the kitchen. Slowly and quietly, he walked across the hall to the kitchen door. He carefully opened it and slipped inside. Sister Margaret Mary was in the pastry room kneading dough. She looked up and saw him. A floured finger rose to her lips and she nodded to him. Charlie understood. He peeked around a wheeled metal rack filled with empty plates and bowls. Sister Patricia was quietly cutting a large meatloaf and placing the slices of meat on platters. She was too focused on her work to notice him. At last, Charlie saw Sister Faith. She was standing by a huge mixer and singing, "Ave Maria, gratia plena, Maria, gratia plena, Maria gratia plena, Ave, Ave, Dominus, Dominus tecum." Charlie recognized the hymn. It was his favorite, Franz Schubert's *Ave Maria*. His grandmother used to sing it to him at bedtime.

A tear came to his eyes as memories of his childhood with his grandmother flooded his mind. Life was good then. They had each other. He wiped his eyes, grateful that the rack hid him from the sisters. He quietly listened until Sister Faith finished. Turning around, he slipped back into the hall.

THANKSGIVING

Fall had definitely arrived. Charlie woke to find the window beside his bed was fogged up and there was a nip in the air. He sat up in his bed and put his bare feet on the floor only to pull them back. The floor was cold.

"You awake, Gus?" he asked.

Charlie heard the bed on the other side of the partition squeak.

"Yes." Gus's voice sounded as though he was about to fall back to sleep.

"Happy Turkey Day," Charlie said.

"It's too early for turkey," Gus groaned.

"How about a fritter and some coffee?"

"Sure. You gonna go get it?"

"No. We're both going to go downstairs and get it. Come on, get up."

"Okay." Gus let out a loud yawn. Charlie could imagine Gus stretching.

He decided to shower before getting dressed. It would give Gus a few extra minutes to wake up. However, when Charlie returned, dressed and ready for breakfast, Gus was still in bed.

"You gonna come, or what?" Charlie asked, standing beside Gus's bunk.

Gus opened his eyes wide. "I'm awake. I'm up," he said while he threw the covers off. Again, he yawned. "What time is it?"

"It's eight o'clock. Sister Margaret Mary is going not going to let us have anything if you don't hurry up." Charlie knew that was a lie. Sister Margaret Mary would always give them something to eat, no matter how late they were. Still, Charlie was anxious to get down stairs.

It took Gus nearly half an hour to get dressed. He moved slower than a sloth, Charlie thought while he paced in the dorm lounge. Finally, he was ready and they headed downstairs.

"I can't wait to see how the sisters have decorated the refectory," Charlie said when they reached the second-floor landing.

"I'm more interested in the food."

"Of course you are," Charlie teased. "Last year we had a buffet. Complete with waffles, scrambled eggs, sausage links, bacon—"

"Stop! Stop!" Gus said. "My stomach is growling."

Both boys laughed.

When they entered the refectory, the joy and anticipation drained from Charlie's face. There were no decorations, no fancy buffet. Everything looked as though it were any other day of the year.

"What's going on?" Charlie asked Ted Wilson, who was seated with two other boys from his dorm.

"You have to get a tray from the kitchen," he said. "They'll explain."

"Okay," Charlie said, sounding bewildered. "Come on, Gus."

Sister Faith greeted the two boys with a big smile and opened arms. "Happy Thanksgiving Day," she said.

"Happy Thanksgiving," Charlie repeated back but sounding anything but happy. "What's going on?"

"Well, this year things are going to be a little different. Instead of the small group of you boys dining alone, you have been invited to dine with the brothers in the abbey's refectory this afternoon."

"Really?" Gus said, sounding a bit fearful.

"Yes," Sister Faith answered. "I bet you would each like a tray. I'll get them ready."

Charlie watched her hurry away. This was not the way the holiday was supposed to go. Dining with the monks did not sound like fun. They would have to be on their best behavior and could not pig out. Charlie was especially worried about Gus. Gus was not the tidiest of eaters.

"Here we go," Sister Faith said, pushing a small cart with two trays on top.

When Charlie saw the trays, it brought a smile to his face. There was a plate with three different types of pastries, another with scrambled eggs, sausage links, and bacon, a bowl of cubed fruit, and a candle in the shape of a turkey.

"Wow," Gus said. "Are there any waffles?"

"Oh," Sister Faith gasped. "I almost forgot." She hurried away and returned with another plate of waffles and a small pitcher of syrup. "There. You should be all set."

"This looks amazing," Charlie said. "I don't think I could eat all of this."

"Well, do your best," she said with a grin and a wink.

Charlie and Gus returned to the refectory, taking the cart with them. Ted was still sitting at the table, but the other two boys had gone.

"So, now you know," Ted said.

"Yeah," Charlie responded.

"At least it's only for one day. Tomorrow we'll be back to normal."

"I'll believe it when I see it," Charlie said. He looked into his empty coffee cup.

"Coffee's over there," Ted said pointing at the table beside the kitchen door. "There's even hot chocolate."

"There is?" Gus said, grabbing his cup and hurrying across the refectory. "There's even whipped cream in a can," he announced before tipping his head back and squirting it into his mouth.

"That's gross," Ted said. "Other people might want to use that, too."

"Rewee?" Gus said with his mouth overflowing.

"I don't," Charlie said.

Gus swallowed the cream and filled his mouth again.

"Say, Charlie, do you think I could talk to you?" Ted asked.

"About what?"

"Not now. Maybe after you eat, you and I could go for a walk?"

"Sure. Everything okay?"

"Yeah," Ted answered but the expression on his face belied his claim.

"Okay," Charlie repeated.

After Charlie had finished eating, he sat back and looked at his tray. He had eaten most of his eggs, a waffle and all of the sausages. Gus took the bacon and one of the sugared doughnuts. Charlie wrapped the fritter and chocolate doughnut to save for later.

"Are we supposed to give this back to the kitchen?" he asked holding the turkey candle.

"No," Ted said, "It's a gift to you from the sisters. We each got one." He held up his candle.

Charlie smiled. "That's so cool." He stood up. "I'll just take my tray back to the kitchen, then we can go, if you like?"

"Sure," Ted said.

Minutes later, after taking his snacks and candle back to his cubicle, Charlie met up with Ted on the front steps.

"Where to?" he asked.

"Oh," Ted said and glanced to his right and left. "This way." He turned right, toward the grotto and cemetery.

"Is everything all right?" Charlie asked.

"I don't know. Do you ever have a feeling like you don't want to be here?"

"Yes," Charlie answered. "I wish I could still be with my grandma."

"No, I mean, here, on this planet?"

Charlie cast Ted a confused look. "Meaning?"

"Sometimes I wonder if things would be better if I weren't around."

"Why would you say that?"

"Because," Ted answered, avoiding eye contact with Charlie and kicking a stone along the walk. "Everything is just too hard. I've got no one outside this abbey. No one who wants me. No one who cares one way or the other. In a little over a year from now, I'm supposed to decide to stay or leave? How can I leave? I'll be alone."

"I see," Charlie said. "But you want to be a priest, don't you?"

"No. I just told them that so I wouldn't have to leave with the others last year. The truth is, I'm scared. I don't know what to do."

"I'm scared, too," Charlie said.

"You are?" Ted said, sounding shocked. "You seem to have it all together."

"It's a front. I'm terrified. Father Cecil keeps asking me what I want to do with my life and I haven't a clue. The thought of leaving here is overwhelming. I mean, where would I live? How will I support myself? It's all too much."

"Exactly," Ted said. "So, what do we do?"

Charlie stopped walking and looked at his schoolmate. "For me, I do a lot of praying, asking God to show me the way."

"I do that, too."

"And as hard as it is, I talk to Father Cecil. You should talk to Brother Simon or one of the monks."

"No. I can't do that," Ted said. "I could never tell them the truth about how I'm feeling or that I lied about wanting to be a priest. They'd send me away like they did the other guys."

Charlie thought about what he just heard. His mind was a blank as to what to do next. "Ted, no matter how scary it may seem, now. It will work itself out. You are smart, talented, and a hard worker. You'll do fine if and when you decide to leave here. But, I for one would really miss you if you...."

Ted's brown eyes teared.

"Promise me, you won't do anything like that."

"Okay," Ted answered.

"Hey, maybe celebrating Thanksgiving with the brothers this afternoon will clear things up for you, and for me." Charlie shoulder bumped Ted. "You really are a good person, a wonderful friend."

"Thanks, Charlie."

The two turned around and headed back to the abbey.

~§~

"Where did you disappear to?" Gus asked Charlie when the boys gathered in the lobby to wait for Brother Simon.

"I went for a walk," Charlie answered.

"With Ted?"

"Part of the time."

"What did he want?"

"Nothing really," Charlie said, purposely trying to be vague and hoping Gus would lose interest in this line of questioning. "What did you do?"

"I had a private rehearsal with Brother Linus. He helped me with my lines and showed me what to do."

"Cool. I have my turn with him tomorrow. Although, he said I'm doing fine. I can't wait for dress rehearsal in two weeks. Did he tell you what your costume will look like? In the movies your character wore a big green robe and a Santa hat."

Gus shook his head. "He said they aren't doing the traditional costumes. Something about them being too close to the monks' habits. Instead, I'll look more like a leprechaun."

"Really?" Charlie said. "I wonder what mine will be."

The door to the monastery wing opened and Brother Simon walked into the foyer. He looked as if he were a twin of Father Vicar; tall, gaunt, dark beady eyes, stern. The only difference was Brother Simon had a softer side that occasionally slipped out. He looked at the boys, taking a silent roll call.

"You're all here. Excellent," he spoke with his chin slightly raised. "You've each been assigned to sit at separate tables with the brothers. This way you will be able to get to know them versus keeping to yourselves. When we enter the refectory, I will escort you to your table and introduce you to the brothers there. It is the expectation that you will use proper table etiquette and respect the brothers. Are we all on the same page?"

"Yes, Brother Simon," they answered.

"Very well, let us go," he said, and started to turn around, but stopped. "One last thing, there is no talking until we reach your table."

Charlie looked at Gus and then took their place in line. Charlie had been to the abbey's refectory many times last summer and with Father Cecil. During the rainy days and cold wintery days, they would sit in the refectory enjoying either coffee or hot cocoa. There was always a supply of shortbread cookies to nibble on, fresh from the abbey's bakery. Charlie liked to dip them into his coffee. He wondered if Gus had ever been to the abbey's refectory.

Brother Simon delivered the boys to their tables and then retreated to his own table. Charlie halfway expected him to sit with one of the students, but he sat with a group of brothers.

Charlie looked at the brothers around him. Across from him was an elderly monk who was hunched over slightly and had trouble keeping his head up. When he spoke, Charlie found he had to strain to hear. The monk's voice was weakened by age. Beside him was a younger monk who seemed to be his helper. He poured a glass of water for the aged one and handed it to him. A strange feeling stirred in Charlie's chest. He was not sure what it was, but it brought a smile to his lips and a tear to his eyes at the same time.

Charlie looked away, at the head table. Father Abbot was not there. Instead, Prior Benedict stood with his hands hidden in his robes. Two other monks stood on either side of him. Without a word of introduction or instruction, he bowed his head and all the monks did the same. Charlie followed their example. Prior Benedict then offered a prayer that seemed to be more of a sermon than grace. When he was finished, he took his seat, and then the rest of those assembled did the same.

"It's so nice of you to join us, Master MacCready," the young brother seated to the right of the elderly monk said while they waited for the server to bring the feast. "My name is Brother Phillip. This is Father Cornelius," he introduced the elderly monk.

"Pleased to meet you," Charlie said.

"I'm Brother Zachary," the one who poured the water said.

Charlie looked to his right.

"I'm Brother Laurance."

"And I'm Father Austin," the monk to Charlie's left said. "So, tell me Master MacCready, are you interested in becoming a member of the abbey?"

"Uh—" Charlie hesitated. Being caught off-guard, he was not sure what to say. "I don't know, yet," he answered.

"Fair enough," Father Austin said. "When I was your age, I wasn't sure either. However, when the call came, I was eager to answer it."

"So, have you been here long?" Charlie asked.

"Do you mean at the abbey or a priest?"

"I guess both."

Father Austin snorted when he smirked. "I came to the abbey when I was fifteen. I joined the order after my sophomore year in college. I was ordained six years later and I've been assigned to a parish ever since."

"Oh," Charlie said. "So, you don't live here full time?"

"No," Father Austin answered while he took a spoonful

of candied yams and put it on his plate. "There is a shortage of priests in the diocese, so several of us have been given parish assignments. For some of us, it is a full-time assignment, and for others it's a weekender."

"I didn't know that." Charlie looked at the other monks.

"Oh, no," Brother Zachary spoke up as though reading Charlie's mind. "Only the priests are given parish assignments. The brothers are given assignments here at the abbey or our priory in Idaho."

"I see."

Charlie listened with keen interest to the stories and histories of each of the brothers. He learned that Father Cornelius served as a chaplain on a Navy ship during World War II. That he had witnessed the horrors of war on the ocean, and after returning to the abbey, it had taken him several years before he would leave the hilltop to go to town. Brother Zachary joined the priory in Idaho and was on temporary assignment to the abbey to assist in the infirmary while Brother James was away. Charlie could not believe he had been there for four years and never knew about the monks' assignments. He had always assumed they stayed at the abbey or at the priory.

That evening, back in the dorm lounge, Gus sat with his feet propped up on the trunk.

"This was the best Thanksgiving ever," he said and then belched. "Oh, sorry." He covered his mouth.

"It was interesting," Charlie said. "I was surprised by how much food there was. I figured they wouldn't have a lot."

"Why's that?" Gus asked.

"I don't' know. I just figured with their vow of poverty and all...."

"Oh, I never thought of that." Gus cocked his head to the side as though he were receiving another thought. "Hey, you want some pumpkin pie? The brothers at my table gave me two extra slices."

"You're joking, right?" Charlie said, putting his hands on his stomach and blowing out his cheeks as though he were about to hurl.

"No," Gus said.

Charlie tilted his head back and closed his eyes. He could not believe Gus was still hungry after the feast they had just eaten.

THE TOWERS

Snow had fallen overnight. When Charlie opened his eyes and looked out his window, he felt as if it were Christmas morning. The edges of the glass pane were frosted. It reminded him of how his grandmother would lightly spray flocking snow around the outer edges of their living room window.

He turned over and looked at his alarm clock. The morning bell was still ten minutes away. Quietly he threw his covers off and sat up on the edge of his bed. The concrete floor felt cold against his bare feet. He quickly found his slippers and put them on. Tiptoeing to his locker, he grabbed his toiletry bag and a towel before heading to the showers.

The hot water felt good against Charlie's skin. He stood with his head bent down and let the water massage his shoulders and back for a while. Turning around, he ducked his head beneath the showerhead.

"Hey, don't use up all the hot water," Howard's voice echoed from the neighboring stall.

Charlie jolted. He wiped the water from his face and opened his eyes. "Howard?"

"Who else were you expecting?" Howard asked and laughed.

"I wasn't expecting anyone."

"You ready for our concert this afternoon at The Towers?"

"Yeah. You?"

"I guess." Howard's answer sounded as if he were underwater. "Hey, I told Father Aloysius we'd give him a hand with setting up the risers and stuff."

"Why'd you do that?" Charlie said.

"It doesn't hurt to keep on his good side."

"Will you two keep it down over there," another voice said from across the shower room.

"Walters, is that you?" Howard said.

"Yes. Now, keep it down. Everyone can hear you in the hallway."

"Oh," Charlie said and ducked his head under the water one last time. He shut off the shower and opened the glass door just enough to grab his towel and not to release the warmth in the shower stall. Closing the door again, he toweled off.

Back in the dorm, he dressed in his black slacks, white shirt and gold bowtie, the uniform for all members of the choir. He glanced at the gold blazer in his locker before grabbing a pair of socks and his shoes. He headed to a chair in the dorm lounge to put them on.

A moment later, Howard rushed into the dorm laughing and with his towel around his waist.

"What's so funny?" Charlie asked.

"Shh!" someone hissed from across the dorm.

Howard ducked and put a finger to his lips while he stifled his laughter. "I got Walters, good," he whispered. "While he was in the shower, I opened the door to his outer stall and took his towel."

"You didn't!" Charlie gasped.

"I did. I put it in the stall beside his. I think Ted Wilson is using it."

"Howard, you are incorrigible."

Howard gave Charlie a puzzled look. "Whatever that

means. Well, I gotta go get dressed. Meet you downstairs for breakfast." He turned around and hurried out of the dorm.

Being Saturday, breakfast was casual and not mandatory. The boys were free to come down to the refectory at their leisure until nine-thirty. There was always coffee and pastries, but for the first hour there were eggs, sausages, bacon, and waffles or pancakes. Charlie looked forward to having sausages with his morning Danish.

He finished tying his shoelaces and retrieved his gold blazer. Before he could go downstairs there was one more thing he needed to do. He headed back to the shower room to return Rick's towel. However, before he could reach the door, it opened and Rick poked his head out.

"Where is he?" Rick was obviously angry and dripping wet.

"Look in the stall beside the one you used," Charlie informed him.

"Why?"

"You'll find your towel."

"Not funny, MacCready," Rick scowled.

"I didn't do it," Charlie said, but Rick had already ducked back inside and the door had closed. He shrugged and continued on his way down to the refectory for breakfast.

The morning bell rang when Charlie reached the stairs. He turned and looked back. The doors to Saint Peter and Saint Thomas opened and a group of boys with towels in hand headed for the showers. They would have to hurry if they didn't want to take a cold shower, Charlie thought while he continued on his way.

"Good morning, Master MacCready," Brother Simon greeted him when he reached the refectory on the first floor.

Charlie jumped and tried to hide being startled but the grin on the assistant dean's face told him he was not successful.

"I see, you're dressed and ready for this afternoon's concert," Brother Simon said, and nodded knowingly.

"Howard just told me he volunteered us to help set up

at The Towers," Charlie said. He put a plate and cup on his tray then he started down the buffet table. Brother Simon followed and filled his coffee before choosing a glazed cruller.

He followed Charlie to a nearby table and took the seat across from him. "Is something troubling you?" he asked, seeing Charlie's somber expression.

"I was just thinking about the old people who live at The Towers. It must be depressing for them."

"Why would you think that?"

"I know my grandmother hates it where she is. She didn't have a say in where she went. My uncle Chester just stuck her in there, away from me, away from her friends. She's all alone."

"You write to her, often, don't you?"

"Yes, almost every other day."

"Then, she's not ignored. She knows how you feel about her and understands why you can't be with her."

"I suppose."

"You know, I bet for those people at The Towers, this is the highlight of their holiday. After the concert, they have asked the boys to stick around and visit with some of the residents. Why don't you join them?"

"I couldn't. I mean, I wouldn't know what to say."

"Sometimes you don't have to say anything, just listen to them. I'm sure you will find they have some fascinating stories to tell."

Charlie took a sip of his coffee. "Okay," he said.

The dining room at The Towers looked festive. The sunflower-yellow walls were draped with green tinsel garlands, making the walls and matching brocade drapes look golden. A ceiling-high artificial Christmas tree decorated with twinkling lights and holiday ornaments stood as a focal point in the corner to the right of the dance floor. The tables were all covered with white tablecloths. A red or green charger plate was placed on the table in front of each chair. In the center of the table was a cheerful centerpiece made with pine and holly sprigs, pine cones, poinsettia flowers and a holiday bow.

Charlie was awestruck as he looked around the room while he helped Howard carry the riser to the dance floor.

"Place it right here, boys," Father Aloysius instructed.

They set the riser on the floor beside the first one and quickly moved out of the way. Two other boys put their heavy load down beside it. There was a flurry of clanking metal, locks sliding into place, and loud banging as the boys set the risers up. Turning them over and connecting them to one another, the three risers formed an arc. Father Aloysius stepped back and had the boys turn the risers until they faced the audience and, more importantly, him.

The chirping from the casters as two of the helpers from The Towers wheeled the upright piano closer caused Charlie to wince. The pitch was sharp and unpleasant but it seemed to go unnoticed by the elderly men. Father Aloysius directed them to where he wanted the piano placed.

Once everything was ready, Howard excused himself and left, leaving Charlie and a couple other boys behind. Charlie stood looking at the large pine wreath with a red bow and a gold toy trumpet that hung on the wall directly over the center of the risers.

"Will you be singing for us today?" a frail voice asked.

Charlie turned around and looked at the stooped, elderly woman. Her hair was white as snow. Her face was crisscrossed with wrinkles. Her eyes were a teary, faded blue. When she smiled, they sparkled.

"Yes, ma'am," he answered.

"That's wonderful. I can hardly wait," she said.

Charlie noticed she was gripping her walker tightly with both hands. He looked at the chairs that lined the walls. "Would you like to sit down?" he asked.

"Would you sit with me?"

"Certainly," Charlie answered without hesitation.

Slowly they walked across the room toward the chairs against the wall, but the woman stopped by one of the tables set for the residents.

"This will do nicely," the woman said, eyeing the Christmas tree nearby. She let Charlie pull out a chair before she released her walker and sat down. Once she was comfortable, Charlie sat on the chair beside her.

"You remind me of my son, when he was a boy," she said. "He had auburn hair, too, you know. He was such a lovely young man. I bet your mother is proud of you."

"I hope so," Charlie said, ignoring the sting he felt in his chest. "So, is your son coming to see you?"

"Oh no," she answered and shook her head ever so slightly. "He has his own family now, three boys and two girls," she said proudly, but then sighed. "Of course, they're all grown up now, with children of their own. They all live just an hour away, but they are very busy, you know."

Charlie felt a tug inside. "Do you have other children?"

"I did," she answered with a pained smile. "A beautiful girl with dark curly hair. I lost her when she was five, along with my husband."

"I'm so sorry," Charlie said.

She patted his hand. "It's okay. It was a long, long time ago. Though, I do tend to think of them now and again. I wonder what she would have become all grown up. I miss my husband, too. Not his drinking, mind you."

"He used to drink?"

"Oh, like a fish," she said with a chuckle. "But I lost him and our little girl because of it. He shouldn't have been driving." She looked away as though lost in a thought. Then with a shake of her head, she was back. "So, what carols will you be singing?"

"We're going to sing *O Holy Night*—"

"Oh, that's my favorite," she interrupted him, sounding happy. "I love that song. I used to sing it to my son when he was little. I haven't sung in years, though. My voice isn't what it used to be, you know. But I do love listening to it."

"I like it, too."

"What else are you singing?"

Charlie listed off a few more songs and listened to her reminisce about Christmases past. Stories about her childhood, baking cookies and pies in a wood-burning oven with her mother, going out in the snow to find the perfect Christmas tree with her father, singing carols while stringing popcorn into garlands. They were her happy memories.

"Excuse me," Father Aloysius said. "It's about time for us to get ready."

"Oh, I'm sorry," the woman said. "I didn't mean to keep you."

"Not at all," Charlie said. "I enjoyed visiting with you. I'll see you after the concert, and you can tell me how we did."

"I'd like that," she said with a smile and a twinkle in her eyes.

"My name is Charlie, by the way," he said.

"I'm Mrs. Iverson." She smiled at him and held out her hand.

Charlie gave her hand a gentle squeeze. It felt cold. He did not expect that, and it jolted him. He smiled at her again before going to join the rest of the choir.

The boys huddled together in the lobby, keeping the hallway clear for the residents. Charlie kept thinking about the Mrs. Iverson while he watched one group after another of white-haired men and women dressed in festive, formal attire enter the dining room. There were several couples but also a few by themselves. Charlie wondered if their stories were the same, abandoned by their children. It made him think of his parents. Would he really abandon them if they showed up now? He looked away from the dining room doors and searched for Howard. Spotting him across the lobby, he started making his way toward him.

"Line up, boys," Father Aloysius said.

Charlie quickly changed course and took his place in line with all the other second bass singers. During the past summer, his voice had dropped even lower, putting him in the group that stood on the top riser. Howard was also in his group, but his place was at the end of the row.

Inside the dining room, someone was speaking into a microphone. Charlie could scarcely make out what he was saying over the crackling and high-pitched feedback in the speakers. The room erupted in applause.

"We're on," Father Aloysius said. "Remember to smile." He turned around and after taking a deep breath, led the boys into the dining room, up the center aisle and to the risers.

Charlie stole a glance at the table to his right as he walked up the aisle. He spotted Mrs. Iverson. She was applauding with the rest of the people at her table and smiling.

Once in place on the top riser, Charlie looked at all the faces staring back at them. All had a look of joyful anticipation. Charlie forced himself to look away before his nerves got the better of him.

Father Aloysius tapped his baton on his music stand. Charlie looked at him and the room disappeared as the lights dimmed. Father Aloysius raised his baton and the pianist began to play. The choir started with an old carol, *It Came Upon A Midnight Clear*, and followed it with *O Holy Night*. Charlie stole a glance at his new friend and saw her lips moving as she silently sang along. When they had finished their ninth song, a freshman boy in the first tenor row at the bottom of the risers stepped forward. The rest of the choir began quietly singing, "rum pum pum pum rum." Then the soloist began singing *The Little Drummer Boy*. Charlie loved this song. There was no piano. Just the boys singing backup. He wished he could hear it from the audience's seats. When they finished their last song, the room was filled with applause.

Before Father Aloysius could lead the boys away, the announcer returned to the microphone. He thanked the choir and then asked if they wouldn't mind joining the tables and having some refreshments with the residents.

"Certainly," Father Aloysius answered for them. "Do you want to assign them to a table?"

"No, no," the announcer said. "Just let them pick a table."

Charlie waited anxiously until he was off the riser. He quickened his pace when he saw another boy heading for the empty chair at the table where his new friend was seated. Luckily, someone at a nearby table called him away and Charlie slipped past him to join his friend.

"Oh wonderful." Mrs. Iverson grinned when she saw Charlie standing by the empty chair beside her. "I was hoping we'd get you."

Charlie smiled and nodded while he looked at the other six residents seated around the large round table.

"Hello," he greeted them. "Do you mind if I join you?"

"Not at all," they answered.

Charlie sat down. "My name is Charlie," he said. "I'm a senior this year at Saint Michael's Seminary High."

"Good for you," a man seated across from him said. "This is Miss Hart, Mr. and Mrs. Engels, I'm Mr. Nottingham, then we have Mrs. Walker and finally Mrs. Iverson."

"We've met," Mrs. Iverson said, and put her hand on Charlie's.

He smiled at her and then looked at the others. "I'm pleased to meet you," he said.

"So, you're wanting to be a priest?" Mr. Nottingham said.

Charlie looked around the table. "I—"

"You'd make a wonderful priest," Mrs. Iverson said. "You're such a kind, caring young man and a good listener."

"Thank you," Charlie said, trying desperately not to blush. "Are you all from around here? I mean, before you moved to The Towers."

"No," Mr. Nottingham said. "I'm from Iowa. Miss Hart, here, is from Boston, is it?"

"Carl, you know perfectly well I'm from Brooklyn, New York," the woman to Charlie's right said, and batted her napkin playfully at the old man.

"We're from town," Mr. Engels said. "We sold our house and decided it was time to pamper ourselves. No more cooking and cleaning, yardwork, and all that. It's time to let others take care of us. Isn't that right, dear?"

Mrs. Engels smiled but had a faraway look in her eyes that left Charlie wondering if she was all right.

"I just moved here from another home, Happy Meadows," Mrs. Walker said.

"You did?" Charlie blurted. "Do you know a woman named Ophelia Zenner?"

Mrs. Walker smiled, and sat back in her chair. "Yes. As a matter of fact, I do."

"You must be the friend my grandma was telling me about. The one who moved."

"Ophelia is your grandmother?" Mrs. Walker asked.

"Yes, she is."

"Oh, she is so proud of you. She talks about you all the time."

Charlie felt his cheeks flush but he did not mind.

"She told me all about your parents, how they abandoned you, you poor thing. She also showed me the Saint Christopher medal and watch she sent you. Do you still have them?"

"Yes," Charlie answered, putting his hand over his chest where the medal hung from the chain.

"That medal was a beautiful work of art," she continued. "May we see it? It's okay, she told me all about it."

"Well," Charlie said, looking nervously around the table. "I suppose it's okay." He pulled the chain from beneath his collar and with it, his key, the locket and the medal.

"You have to see this," she said to the others around the table. "Go ahead, take it off and pass it around so the others can have a closer look."

Not completely sure he should, Charlie slipped the chain over his head. He unclasped it and slipped the key from the chain. Securing the clasp again, he handed the locket and medal to Mrs. Iverson.

"What's this?" she asked, holding the locket.

"It was my mother's locket. It has a picture of her and my dad from a long time ago."

"Is that so?" She looked at him with questioning eyes.

"Yes, my grandmother gave it to me when I lived with her and my grandpa," he said and hoped that would be enough of the story for them.

"May I open it?" she asked.

"Sure," Charlie said as she popped it open.

"What a lovely couple they are. Here, take a look." She handed the locket and medal to Mrs. Walker.

"Oh lovely," she said, giving only a passing glance at the locket. "Yes, this is it. This is the one," she said turning the medal over and looking at the etching on the back. "Did you figure out what the message is on the back?"

Charlie silently gasped. He looked around the table at their inquiring faces. "Yes," he answered.

"Your grandmother said you were a bright boy," she said.

"Well, don't hog it all to yourself, Iris, let the rest of us have a look," Mr. Nottingham said, reaching for the medal.

Iris reluctantly relinquished it and sat with her hands in her lap beneath the table.

"How on earth could you read this? I can barely make out anything," he said squinting at the back of the medal. "It's all but worn off."

"It wasn't easy," Charlie said. "I had a devil of a time but I had a little help."

"Well, you have better eyes than me, young man," he said and passed it along.

The other three made a cursory glance at it.

"Here," Iris jumped up from her seat. "Let me help you

with that." She took the chain and medal from Mrs. Engels and stepped behind Charlie. She unclasped the chain and put it around Charlie's neck before returning to her chair. Charlie quickly tucked his treasures beneath his shirt.

"I noticed you took an old key off the chain," Mr. Nottingham said. "What's the significance of it?"

"Oh, is it a treasure, too?" Iris asked, watching Charlie a bit too intently for his comfort.

"It's really nothing. It's just an old key my grandma had lying around. I liked it so I put it on my chain," he said, uncomfortable with their questions and Mrs. Walker's keen interest in his treasures.

"Master MacCready," Father Aloysius said, standing behind him. "It's time to go."

"So soon?" Mrs. Iverson said, with a bit of sadness.

"I'm afraid so," Father Aloysius said as kindly as he could. Father Aloysius was not known as being gentle. In fact, over the course of his time in the choir, Charlie had witnessed Father Aloysius's temper on many occasions.

"It was wonderful meeting all of you," Charlie said while he rose to his feet.

"You will come visit me again?" Mrs. Iverson asked, grabbing his hand while he scooted the chair back up to the table.

"Yes, I will," he answered. "I promise."

A few minutes later Charlie sat on the bus waiting for the other boys to board. He was cold, and watched the fog from his breath disappear in front of him. "Do you think it can get any colder in here?" he groused while he shivered.

"Probably," Howard said while seated beside Charlie. He leaned into the aisle. "Can we get some heat in here?"

"Patience, Mister Miller," Brother Simon, said, sounding stern. He turned the key in the ignition again and reluctantly the old bus engine started up.

Howard sat back. "So, what'd you think of all those raisins."

"Raisins?" Charlie said.

"Yeah, all those old and wrinkly people."

"That's not nice to call them that," Charlie said, frowning at him.

"I didn't say it to their faces," Howard said. "That would be rude."

The bus suddenly lurched forward and stopped when the engine died. Brother Simon tried to start it again. The engine protested and refused to start. He tried again and it backfired but came to life.

"They're really nice," Charlie said. "But one of them made me uncomfortable."

"Why? Did she make a pass at you?" Howard teased.

"No!" Charlie answered and leaned away from his friend. "Why would you say that?"

Howard did not answer. He just laughed.

"She said she knows my grandmother," Charlie continued. "She even knew about the medal and pocket watch. She said my grandmother showed them to her before sending them to me."

"Really?"

"I guess," Charlie shrugged. "That's what she claimed. She even asked if she could see it again."

"Did you?"

Charlie shrugged. "What could I do? I mean, they were all looking at me. I had to show them."

"No, Charlie."

"It doesn't matter anymore. I've already solved the mystery."

"I know but...." Howard shook his head.

"What's the harm? Besides, I took the key off," Charlie said and took the key out of the inside breast pocket of his blazer. He pulled the chain from beneath his shirt and immediately noticed his locket was missing. "Oh no!" he said. as panic set in. He patted himself down, feeling for the locket in case it was caught by his belt. "No."

"What's the matter?" Howard asked, turning to look at Charlie.

"It's gone."

"The medal?"

"No, my locket. It's not on my chain."

"What? How?"

"Let me out," he said as he tried to stand up. The bus rocked and slid against the curb.

"Sit down, MacCready," Brother Simon shouted over his shoulder while he struggled with the steering wheel.

"But—" Charlie sat down and looked out the window at snow covered ground. "I'll never find it," he said.

"We'll find it," Howard said, trying to sound hopeful but Charlie could hear he was not so positive. "When did you see it last?"

"It was after everyone at the table looked at the medal. Mrs. Walker helped me put it back on—you don't think she took it?"

"What would she want with your locket?" Howard asked.

"I don't know. I don't think it was special. I mean I've found what the key was for."

"I seriously doubt she took it. Perhaps it just fell off somewhere. We can search the bus when we get to the abbey. If we don't find it, we can call the front desk at The Towers and see if anyone turned it in."

"Okay," Charlie said and settled back down again. He could not stop wondering if there was some hidden message in the locket, some clue to where his parents were, that he had not noticed.

The bus bounced and shimmed as it made its way up the slight incline to the road, leaving The Towers behind. Brother Simon turned left and continued to steer the bus along the slippery pavement. When he turned right, onto the abbey's long drive, the bus began to slide off the road. Brother Simon turned the wheel and righted the bus and it continued up the hill to the abbey at the top.

The bus slowed to a stop beneath the portico in front of the abbey. Brother Simon kept the engine running while the boys disembarked.

"You, too, Master Miller and Master MacCready," he said looking in the rearview mirror.

"Just a second, Brother, Charlie lost his locket," Howard said.

"What?" Brother Simon's voice raised. His eyes looked wide in the mirror.

"It must have dropped off my chain," Charlie said. He knelt down and searched the floor beneath the seats.

Howard searched the aisle from back to front and back again. "I don't see it anywhere."

"I'll call The Towers once I put the bus away," Brother Simon said.

"Okay," Charlie said.

"Don't worry, son, we'll find it," Brother Simon said. "Now, get off my bus and go inside."

"Yes, Brother Simon," the boys said.

They left the bus and headed up to their dorms. Charlie was beginning to feel sick. Disappointment, anger, frustration—all kept his stomach churning.

"It'll be okay, Charlie. Brother Simon will find it for you."

"It's gone for good, I just know it," Charlie said.

"Give him a chance."

"What if it held the answer to where my parents are or to something else?"

"Maybe your grandmother knows?"

"No, if it did, she would have told me," Charlie said, as depression set in. "It's just that the locket belonged to my mom. It's all I had of her."

"I'm really sorry," Howard said as they reached the fourth floor.

"I think I want to be alone," Charlie said when they

opened the fire doors.

"Are you sure?"

"Yes. I'll see you at dinner."

Once back in his cubicle, Charlie took his writing tablet from the desk drawer and grabbed a pen. He plopped down in his soft chair in the corner and wrote a letter to his grandmother. He told her about The Towers and the concert, about meeting Mrs. Iverson and how he felt bad for her because she was all alone. He also told her that Mrs. Walker was there and she seemed really nice. Finally, he mentioned losing his locket.

OPENING NIGHT

A week passed. Abbot Ambrose had returned to the abbey, but would not share where he had gone when Charlie informed him about losing the locket. The abbot's lack of concern over the locket being lost led Charlie to believe there was no hidden mystery around it. Still, it bothered Charlie that it was gone, but there was no time to dwell on it. There was something more pressing on his mind. It was opening night for the play, and the butterflies in his stomach were out in full force.

"Sit still," Sister Ann said as she applied black makeup to Charlie's face.

"Sorry."

"I know you're nervous, but stop jittering. You have nothing to worry about. You were sensational at last night's dress rehearsal. You'll do just fine."

Charlie took a deep breath to try to calm his nerves. It did not work. He looked at his costume, hanging on the rack in front of him. The brothers objected to the traditional Grim Reaper robe for Christmas Future because it too closely resembled their habits. Instead, Brother Linus chose a vintage cemetery caretaker's uniform—a long, knee-length, tailored black coat, black slacks, black shirt and black tie, black gloves, and a top hat. Brother Linus wanted Christmas Future to appear as a shadow when on stage. This costume, Brother Linus assured Charlie, would do just that. Charlie wished he could see for himself.

"Now, when you get dressed, be careful not to touch your face," Sister Ann cautioned. "The makeup takes a while to dry. Oh, and don't forget to squint. Brother Linus doesn't want the whites of your eyes to show up."

Charlie squinted.

"Perfect. Do that," Sister Ann said.

Brother Linus walked up just as Charlie stood. "Here, I want you to put this over your head before you put on your top hat." He handed Charlie a black sheer scarf. "This way it will help the illusion of being a shadow and ensure the whites of your eyes won't be seen."

"Do you still want me to squint?"

"Yes," Brother Linus said.

"Okay," Charlie said.

Once dressed, Charlie checked his reflection in the full-length mirror that hung on the wall in the dressing room. At first, he did not recognize himself. Then, the more he stared at his reflection, he liked the way he looked. The fitted coat made him look taller and thinner. He straightened his back and held his head up. The image of Father Vicar flashed in his mind.

"Quit hogging the mirror, Charlie," Rick said, trying to check out his makeup and costume.

"Sorry," Charlie said. He slipped out the door and went to the backstage lounge to wait with the rest of the cast.

The noise from the growing audience made its way backstage. Charlie tried to ignore it but it was becoming increasingly difficult. He wished for the play to be over.

"All those in Act One, places," Sister Ann called out.

A group of actors hurried out of the waiting room.

Charlie put his gloved hand on his stomach and tried once again to calm the butterflies.

The music began. It was showtime. Charlie listened at

the door. The audience was quiet but every once in a while, he could hear them laugh at the appropriate time.

"Master Kuegle," Sister Ann said when she returned to the room. "You're on next."

"Oh-h-h," Gus groaned.

"You'll do fine. Relax," Charlie said as Gus left the room.

Charlie began to run through his scene, acting it out in the small space while he listened to the voices in his head. Nod twice, shake head and turn. Walk to center stage. Turn, point, back away out of the spotlight. "Easy," he said out loud.

"Master MacCready, it's your turn."

Charlie followed Sister Ann to stage left where he waited in the wings for the lights to dim. Once they did, he followed the glow in the dark dots to his place by Scrooge's large four-poster canopy bed. Standing beside the bed, on his mark, Charlie could make out the white curtains. He gently pulled it back to be able to see the sleeping Scrooge.

There was the sound of a clock striking three. The spotlight slowly came on. A woman in the audience gasped, reawakening Charlie's butterflies. Scrooge said his first line. Charlie nodded. He felt his knees begin to go weak. He stiffened his legs. Scrooge said his next line. Charlie nodded and his lower back began to give. He started to bow. Scrooge said his third line. Charlie slowly shook his head and turned away. As he did, his back became stronger and he stood straight. He led Scrooge to center stage.

Moments later, backstage again, Charlie collapsed onto a chair. His legs and hands trembled.

"How'd it go?" Gus asked.

"It was amazing," Charlie gushed. "Did you hear a woman in the audience gasp?"

"She didn't gasp," Gus said. "She screamed."

"Really?" Charlie said, confused about what he heard. "Anyway, my back started to give out, but I recovered and I don't think anyone noticed."

"My knees were shaking the whole time I was onstage," Gus said. "I'm so glad it's over."

"What do you mean, over? We have four more shows to do," Charlie said.

"Don't remind me."

The applause was deafening when the cast took their final bow at the end.

Howard met Charlie backstage. "You were fantastic, creepy, but fantastic."

"How did I look?"

"Like a shadow. Even at the end when you took a bow with the others. You should see yourself."

"That's impossible."

Howard laughed. "Yeah, I guess so."

"Hey, did Mrs. Iverson make it?"

"Yes," Howard answered. "I showed her to her seat. After the show, she had to leave with the rest of the people from The Towers. She told me to tell you she loved it."

Charlie grinned.

"Oh, that is so creepy," Howard said and grimaced. "Don't do that again."

"Why?" Charlie laughed.

"May I have your attention," Brother Linus shouted above the din of excited chatter. The cast hushed. "I just want to tell you how proud I am of all of you. You did an amazing job tonight. Tomorrow, we do a matinee at one. So, I want you all dressed and ready no later than twelve forty-five. Once you have returned your costumes to the rack, you are free to go."

The cast dispersed.

"Well, I best get out of this costume and into the shower," Charlie said. "If last night was any sign, I'm going to have to scrub a long time to get this makeup off."

It was nearly ten-thirty when Charlie emerged from the shower room. The makeup was gone, but his face was pink from scrubbing. Howard was waiting in the lounge. When he saw Charlie, he jumped up from his chair and met him before the shower room door had time to close.

"I almost forgot to tell you," he said. "Mrs. Iverson wanted me to give you this." He handed Charlie a note.

"What is it?"

"I don't know, she didn't say. She just said to give it to you."

Charlie opened the small envelope and took out the piece of paper. He read it to himself first and then looked at Howard. "Listen to this," he said. "I heard about your missing locket. I know who took it. Come see me when you can." Charlie folded the note. "So, I didn't lose it. It was stolen. I bet I know by whom, too."

"That's great, but when can you get away?"

"Maybe after tomorrow's matinee and before the dinner," Charlie said as he thought out loud.

"I'll go with you."

"Thanks."

~§~

After the matinee was finished, Charlie quickly showered and dressed. He met Howard on the front steps of the abbey.

"You didn't get all the black off your face," Howard said.

"Where?" Charlie asked and looked for something to show his reflection.

"There's still a little bit along your hairline, here," he said and touched Charlie's face above his sideburns.

"Well, it'll have to do for now. We only have an hour and a half before we have to be back here for dinner."

The boys headed across the Great Lawn. It took them fifteen minutes to reach The Towers at the bottom of the hill. Both were a bit winded and sweaty.

The lobby in The Towers was surprisingly quiet. There was a faint sound of Christmas music playing over the speakers in the ceiling but aside from the receptionist, no one was around. Charlie approached the front desk. The receptionist, a pleasant looking middle-aged woman with a touch of gray in her hair, smiled at him.

"Welcome, are you here to see someone?" she asked.

"Yes," Charlie answered. "I'd like to see Mrs. Iverson. Is she busy?"

"Mrs. Iverson?" the woman repeated. She looked at a sheet of paper, then picked up the receiver of the phone. She dialed four digits and waited. "Yes, this is the front desk, I have a Mister—" She looked at Charlie.

"Charlie MacCready from Saint Michael's," he said.

"Charlie MacCready from Saint Michael's Abbey here to see you," the woman said into the phone. "Yes, I'm sure. Okay, I'll tell him." She hung the receiver back on the base. "She wanted me to tell you she will be right down. You may wait in our dining room. We have cookies, fruitcakes, and other goodies there. Also, hot cocoa and coffee, too," she said looking behind Charlie at Howard. "Help yourselves."

"Thank you," Charlie said and gave her a nod.

The two boys walked across the lobby to the double doors that had been propped open. A long table was set up down the center of the room with platters and dishes of treats, just as the receptionist described. Howard grabbed a plate and helped himself to the cookies. He bit off the head of a gingerbread man before pouring himself a cup of coffee.

"You want one?" he asked Charlie.

"I'll get it. Thank you," Charlie said and waited until Howard was finished. Once he had his coffee, he followed Howard to a nearby table by the Christmas tree and sat down. It was not long before Mrs. Iverson appeared in the doorway. Charlie left the table and met her.

"What a lovely surprise. When my telephone rang I couldn't for the life of me imagine who would be calling. It's so nice of you to stop by."

Charlie was puzzled by her reaction, since she had

given Howard the note. He guided her by the buffet table. "Would you like something to drink and maybe a snack?"

She eyed the goodies set out on plates with paper doilies. "Well, maybe one of those," she said pointing at an iced sugar cookie.

Charlie grabbed a small plate and napkin. He put one of the cookies onto the plate.

"Oh, and maybe one of those," Mrs. Iverson pointed to another platter of cookies. Charlie added one to her plate. "And a slice of fruitcake." She giggled and covered her mouth. "That's not too much, is it?"

"No," Charlie said and matched her laugh. "How about some coffee or hot chocolate?"

"Do they have tea?" she asked and searched up and down the table.

"I don't know, but I could ask."

"No, I don't want to impose," she said.

"It's no trouble at all. Let me help you to the table and I'll just ask."

A few minutes later, Charlie returned with a cup of hot water and a fresh tea bag. "Here you go," he said as he set it on the table before her. "Where did Howard go?" He looked around the room.

"He said he had to go to the boys' room and would be right back."

Charlie sat down beside her. "How did you like the play last night?"

"Oh, it was wonderful. Except when that last ghost appeared. I'm afraid it startled me and I let out a shriek."

"That was you?" Charlie said.

"I'm afraid so," she said, tilting her head and looking a bit embarrassed.

"I was the ghost on stage. I heard you," Charlie said with a grin.

"It was? I saw your name on the program but I didn't recognize you."

"My face is painted black and covered."

"Oh, that explains it."

"Uh, Mrs. Iverson, Howard gave me your note. The one about my missing locket."

"Oh. Yes, yes."

"You said you know who took it."

She leaned closer to him. "Mrs. Walker stole it."

Charlie recoiled and looked at her. "Really? How do you know?"

"Because at supper the next day, she was wearing a new locket. She was showing it to everyone and saying that her son bought if for her. I knew right away she was lying. She complains about her son all the time. He never comes to visit. He missed her birthday. He didn't do—oh, just the usual gripes we old folks complain to each other about. But in her case, her son died four years ago. There's no way he would have bought her a locket, and an old looking one at that."

"Did she show you what was inside?" Charlie asked.

"Heavens no. When I asked her, she seemed to get flustered. She said she hadn't put anything in it yet. I know it's your locket. I recognized it," she said and nodded while she bit into the sugar cookie.

"I sure wish I could see it. I'd know if it was mine."

"Trust me, it is. Tell you what," she said and leaned closer again. "I'll see if I can't get my hands on it for you."

"Oh, I couldn't ask you to do that," Charlie said.

"You didn't. It's my idea," she said and smiled.

"What'd I miss?" Howard said when he returned to the table.

"I'll tell you on the way back," Charlie said. "We best be going. It was good seeing you again."

"I'll get a note to you when I have the you-know-what," she said and winked.

"Okay," Charlie said. He started to clear the table but she stopped him.

"Leave your dishes. There's a girl who comes in to take

care of all that."

"If you're sure."

"I am."

Charlie started for the foyer.

"Hang on a sec," Howard said, grabbing a napkin. "I just want to take a brownie and another one of these sugar cookies for the road."

On the way back up the hill to the abbey, Charlie told Howard everything that Mrs. Iverson had said. Even about her getting the locket from Mrs. Walker.

"I don't know, Charlie. It all sounds strange. Why would that old lady take it and make up a story about her dead son?"

"Who knows? Maybe she's a bit senile?"

"And another thing, how can Mrs. Iverson get the locket away from Mrs. Walker without her noticing? They live in separate apartments, don't they?"

"As far as I know."

"You know what I think," Howard said. "She's using your missing locket as a way to get you to come see her. You said so yourself, she's lonely. I knew giving her a ticket to the play last night was a bad idea."

"She did enjoy it though," Charlie said.

~§~

At the cast party Sunday night, after their final performance, Charlie sat at a table in the refectory with a cup of fruit punch. Across the room Brother Linus was merrily talking with Mrs. Cratchit and one of the old solicitors. In real life the couple were married. Charlie watched Brother Linus with keen interest. He looked so happy when he was talking about the play. There was a sparkle in his eyes that otherwise was not there. Charlie wondered how Brother Linus could have given up something that obviously brought him so much joy to become a monk? It did not make sense to him.

Later, when most of the cast had left, Brother Linus poured himself a cup of punch and made his way across the room to Charlie's table. "Mind if I sit down?"

"No, not at all," Charlie said.

"I just wanted to tell you, if you haven't heard it already, you did a fantastic job. That part was perfect for you."

"Thank you," Charlie said and felt his cheeks blush. "I thought everyone was good."

"Yes, they were," Brother Linus agreed. "I couldn't have asked for a better cast to work with."

"May I ask you a question?" Charlie said.

Brother Linus looked at him. "Sure."

"I've been watching you. You seem different, so happy when you're talking about the play. Do you ever miss performing?"

"Not entirely. Sure, it was fun, don't get me wrong. I had some great times and acted in some really good shows. But at the end of the day, when one show was finished, it was hurry up and find your next one because there were bills to pay and I had to eat. Sometimes the jobs were few and far between. I don't miss that struggle."

"Why did you give it up to become a monk?"

"Ah," Brother Linus said, leaning back in his chair. "One day I found myself in Saint Patrick's Cathedral in Brooklyn. I had a really rough two years without a show. My life was falling apart in other ways, too. After praying, I had an overwhelming feeling of calmness, that everything was going to be all right. As I was leaving, I noticed a flyer in the vestibule about a retreat at The Priory of the Son in Idaho. I figured, why not? So, I packed my bags and left New York. During that week at the priory, I had what some people would say was a calling. I say it was more like an epiphany. I knew what I was meant to do and where I belonged. Does that make sense?"

"Sort of," Charlie said.

"Have you experienced something similar?"

"No. I still don't know what I'm supposed to do."

"What about what you want to do?"

Charlie shook his head. "I don't know that either."

"Well, you're young. There's time. Don't force it." Brother Linus looked at his watch. "Well, my dear Ghost of Christmas Future, it's time for you to get upstairs to bed. You have classes tomorrow."

"Okay. Thanks for talking with me. Good night." Charlie put his glass on the cart with the other used dishes and headed upstairs.

He was still thinking about his conversation with Brother Linus when he crawled into bed. Turning onto his side, he looked out the window. The outside lights on the gymnasium silhouetted the trees on the Great Lawn. He smiled to himself as he thought about the play. It was fun being a part of it. Then thoughts of his parents crept back into his mind. He wondered what they would have thought had they been there to see him. He pushed the thought away and turned his back toward the window. Closing his eyes, he fell asleep.

MRS. IVERSON

Charlie sat at the bleachers in the gymnasium watching the parents and students visit after the choir's final concert. He envied the boys whose parents came to hear them sing and wondered what it would have been like if his parents had been in the audience. He felt for the locket around his neck then remembered it was not there.

"Hey, there you are," Howard said, walking up the steps to where Charlie was sitting. "What are you doing up here?"

"Nothing," Charlie answered. "Just sitting here watching everyone. What's up?"

"My dad's ready to leave. Are you sure you won't change your mind and come with us for the holidays?"

"Yes. I'm fine. You should celebrate Christmas with your family. Plus, I couldn't leave Gus alone."

"Yeah, I figured as much. I left a present for you and one for Gus under the tree in the lounge," Howard said and stood up.

Charlie stood up as well. "I left yours on your bed with your bag," he said.

"Yeah, I noticed. Thanks."

"Have a merry Christmas," Charlie said and gave

Howard a hug.

"Back at you. I'll see you in two weeks," Howard said before hurrying off to meet up with his father.

"Yeah," Charlie said and started down the steps.

After all the boys and their parents were gone, Charlie began helping the brothers clear the refreshment tables. He put the partial trays of uneaten cookies onto the tiered bakery rack. The empty platters and punch bowls were placed into the waiting tubs to be taken to the dishwasher. Once the tables were cleared and the tablecloths tossed into the laundry basket, Charlie helped Brother Linus fold the tables. Together they returned them to their cupboard beneath the bleachers. It was not hard work but Charlie felt as though he needed a break. He stood back and watched the brothers fold up the huge canvas tarps that protected the hardwood floor. Those, too, were stored beneath the bleachers. Once they finished, Charlie headed back to the abbey.

He was halfway across the Great Lawn when he heard Brother Simon's voice calling him. He stopped and waited for the assistant dean to catch up with him.

"I was hoping I'd catch you," Brother Simon said. "Why don't we sit over there." He directed Charlie to a bench at the edge of a frozen pond. "There's something I need to talk to you about."

"Okay," Charlie said. "Did I do something wrong?"

"No, no, it's nothing like that."

Charlie sat down on the bench and immediately felt its coldness penetrate the thin barrier of his slacks. He fought the urge to jump up.

Brother Simon sat down beside Charlie. His thick wool cape buffered him from the cold.

"You did a fine job both singing and helping the brothers," he said.

There was something different about Brother Simon's voice that caught Charlie's ear. He had heard it before but it had been a long time.

"You're welcome?" Charlie said, not sure how to respond to the compliments.

Brother Simon's lips curled slightly and then flattened. "Son, you remember the elderly woman you spoke to at The Towers?"

"Mrs. Iverson?" Charlie said.

Brother Simon nodded. "Yes, Mrs. Iverson. Son, I'm sorry to tell you, she passed away last night."

"She wha—" Charlie's voice gave out. Tears instantly filled his eyes, blurring his vision.

"I'm sorry," Brother Simon said.

"Why? What happened?" Charlie asked, his voice squeaking as his vocal cords tightened. He wiped the tears from his cheeks.

"She was old, son, ninety-four. She slipped away in her sleep. This morning one of the caregivers found her."

Charlie heard what Brother Simon said but did not really comprehend it. Instead, Charlie was thinking about her family. How they did not want anything to do with her while she was living. Now they could bury her and be rid of her for good. He became angry with them.

"The front desk gave me this for you. Mrs. Iverson left it with them for you," Brother Simon said and took an envelope from the pocket in his habit. He held it in front of Charlie. "Go ahead and take it."

Charlie took the envelope and felt it had something hard inside. He opened it. There was a note. He took it out and quietly read it to himself.

Charlie, Merry Christmas. Your friend, Mrs. Iverson

Charlie looked in the envelope and saw a gold locket. He took it out to get a better look. "It's not mine," he said. "It's the wrong locket."

"What are you talking about?"

"Mrs. Iverson told me she heard about my missing

locket. She said the following day or so Mrs. Walker showed her a locket claiming her son had just given it to her. According to Mrs. Iverson, Mrs. Walker's son died four years ago. This must be her locket." Charlie handed it back to Brother Simon.

"I see," he said, staring at the trinket in his hand. He shoved it back into his pocket. "Are you okay?"

"I will be," Charlie said.

"Come on, let's get you inside where it's warm."

The two returned to the abbey.

~§~

Christmas morning arrived with a bang. Gus had kicked the partition that separated his cubicle from Charlie's when he jumped out of bed. The sudden noise jolted Charlie from a good dream but once awake, he could not remember it.

"Sorry about that," Gus called over the partition.

"No problem," Charlie said and yawned. He stretched, then rolled over to look at the clock. It was seven in the morning. "Why are you up so early?" he groaned and rolled over onto his back.

"It's Christmas!" Gus said, sounding like his character from the play.

"Big deal," Charlie answered. He looked at the window beside his bed. Snow was falling. Curious, Charlie sat up and looked down at the ground. It was covered in a blanket of white. He could feel excitement beginning to bloom in his chest.

"Come on. Let's go see what the others are doing," Gus said, standing at the foot of Charlie's bed. "Grab your robe."

Charlie hesitated for a moment. He looked at Gus dressed in pajamas and a bathrobe, and with a huge grin on his face. He knew Gus was not going to let him stay in bed.

"Okay," Charlie said, and threw off his covers. He grabbed his robe that was draped over the chair at his desk and followed Gus out of the dorm.

A table was set up beneath the bulletin board. On it was

a platter of pastries, another of festively decorated iced sugar cookies, gingerbread men, and butter cookies, a pitcher of orange juice, and two carafes of hot coffee. Charlie took one of the mugs and filled it with coffee. He looked at the pastries for a maple bar, but seeing none, settled for a glazed cruller. He turned around and saw Ted and Dale sitting on the sofa in front of the Christmas tree. They each were cradling a coffee mug in their hands.

"Hi guys, Merry Christmas," he greeted as he walked around the pool table to the center of the lounge.

"Hey, Charlie, Gus," Ted said.

Dale smiled and nodded.

"So, what do you suppose is under the tree?" he asked as he sat down in one of the overstuffed chairs.

"D-d-don't know," Dale answered.

"We have to wait until the others wake up," Ted said. "I'm gonna get another doughnut. You want anything?"

"C-c-coffee," Dale said, holding out his mug.

"Sure." Ted took Dale's cup and headed across the room to the table.

"Grab me a napkin, please," Charlie called.

It was nearly nine o'clock when the last of the boys arrived in the lounge with Father Mark and Brother Simon. They grabbed something to drink and a pastry from the table, then found a place to sit on the floor in front of the tree. Father Mark crouched down and began handing out the gifts.

"Master MacCready," he said, looking at the tag on a small, thin present wrapped in gold foil. "This one is for you."

"Thank you," Charlie said. He looked at the tag but only saw his name written on it. He turned the gift over and over. "Father, who is this from?"

"I don't know," Father Mark said, while handing a gift to Dale. "It doesn't say. Simon?"

"This is the first I've seen of it. It was not in the box with the other gifts," Brother Simon said. "Open it. Perhaps there's a note inside."

Charlie looked at the tag again, then carefully unwrapped the box. Beneath the wrapping paper was a thin square box. Gently Charlie lifted the top off. Inside was a square cotton pad with a gold chain. "Wow!" he said and held it up.

"A chain?" Father Mark asked. "Nice."

When Charlie lifted the chain, he dropped the box and a note fell out onto the floor. He quickly picked it up.

Father Mark said. "What's that?"

Charlie unfolded the paper. The writing was small. Charlie squinted to read it. "It's a note. It says, I heard you lost your locket. Thought you could use a new chain."

"That's all?" Brother Simon asked.

"Yes, there's no signature."

"That was nice of whoever," Father Mark said, not sounding the least bit concerned.

Charlie returned the chain to the box and closed it.

"Here's another gift," Brother Mark said when he handed Charlie a slightly larger package wrapped in paper with green holly and red berries printed on it. "This one is from Howard."

"Thank you," Charlie said and blushed. He opened the box. Inside was a black leather wallet. He looked inside and found a dollar and a note. "Seed money to grow some more," it read in Howard's scrawl. Charlie smiled and put the wallet back in the box.

Father Mark handed Charlie another present. "This one is from me," he said.

"Thank you." Charlie opened it carefully, feeling a bit awkward knowing that Father Mark was watching them. He glanced at Gus and saw the package of socks. He looked at Ted and noticed a prayer book. He looked at his own gift, a Bible with a black leather cover and gold letters. His mouth dropped open. He looked at Father Mark who was smiling at him. "Thank you," he said.

"This one's from me," Brother Simon said, handing him a small neatly wrapped gift.

Charlie opened it. His eyes widened and he took out a crucifix on a chain and held it up in the light. It looked like the one Abbot Ambrose wore. "Are you sure?" he said to Brother Simon.

"Yes," he answered.

"Gee, thank you."

Charlie's final gift was from his grandmother. It was a book with an embossed brown leather cover and ribbon marker. In the lower right corner were the letters CM entwined. He opened the book but the lined pages were all blank. He carefully turned to the first page and read a note from his grandmother.

Here is a journal for you to record special days and events in your life. Keep it to reflect on when you are older.

Charlie closed the book and placed it with his other gifts. He picked up the wrapping papers and folded them into neat little squares. Collecting the ribbons and bows, he tied them around the gift wrap to store them in the shoe box where he kept his other momentos.

"I think I will put my things away," he said and excused himself.

"Don't be too long, Master MacCready," Brother Simon said. "The sisters have prepared a proper brunch for us in the refectory."

"I won't be long," Charlie said.

Alone in his cubicle, he took out the note from the gold chain and reread it. There was something that looked familiar about it, though he didn't know why. His first thought was Rick. Rick wrote small and he certainly would know about the locket. However, Rick was not the generous type. He would never spend the money on a present like the that.

Charlie glanced at the program from the play. After the final performance he had the members of the cast sign it for him. He picked it up and looked at the signatures. He felt a jolt run through him when he noticed Brother Linus's writing. He held up the gift note and compared the two.

"No," Charlie said, confused by what he was seeing. "Why would he?"

He put the note back in the box with the chain and tucked it into the drawer of his desk. He rushed to his locker and quickly changed into his uniform.

~§~

"I see you've figured it out," Brother Linus said, holding the door of his cell open and looking at Charlie.

"Yes," Charlie said. "Thank you so much, but why?"

"Why did I give it to you or why didn't I sign it?"

"Both, I suppose."

"Let's take a little walk." Brother Linus stepped into the hallway and closed his cell door. Silently he walked beside Charlie to the back stairs and down to the first floor. Once there, he directed Charlie to the cloister garden door.

Snow was still falling in light, tiny flakes. It covered the bare branches of the ornamental cherry trees, the statues, benches, and birdbaths. Slowly, Brother Linus began walking along the path around a frozen pond.

"I didn't sign it because I hoped to remain anonymous," he said. "I didn't want to draw attention to myself, but now I see, you are too clever. How did you figure it out?"

"I looked at your signature on my program," Charlie said.

"Oh, how silly of me. I had forgotten I signed it. I signed so many for people." Brother Linus sighed and shook his head.

"But, why would you give me such an expensive present?"

Brother Linus stopped and turned to face Charlie. "I guess you remind me of myself. I remember when I was your age. I was afraid to leave Julliard. New York was a huge city filled with cold and unfriendly strangers and except for the handful of kids I knew from school, I knew no one. Julliard was safe. It was home. I didn't want to leave it.

"Charlie, you're at that same stage in your life. You have to decide what you are going to do with your life. If you leave, what will you do to earn a living? Where will you live? There is so much to consider." Brother Linus resumed walking around the cloister pond.

"When I finally first left Julliard, I felt lost. Like a proverbial fish out of water. I secured a small apartment, even smaller than my cell if you can imagine. Then I got a job as a dishwasher in an Italian restaurant at night. I went on auditions during the day and, at first, it was always the same thing, you're too tall, too short, too thin, you're just not what we're looking for. I began to wonder if I had wasted my time at Julliard. It took almost a year before I was cast as an extra in *Hair* and after that in *Cabaret*. Things seemed to open up after that. I landed the role as one of the disciples in a new musical called *Godspell*. It wasn't a major role. I was mostly in the background. The show received rave reviews and everyone in the cast got a career boost. After that show closed, I quickly landed a role in another religious musical, *Jesus Christ Superstar*. The last show I performed in was *You're A Good Man Charlie Brown*. However, during one performance, I twisted my ankle and was replaced. After that, the jobs dried up. The restaurant where I had worked as a dishwasher, closed so I was out of a job. I lived off my savings while I looked for work, but there seemed to be nothing. My lease on the apartment was up. That's what led me to Saint Patrick's."

"That's awful," Charlie said. "I had no idea."

"How could you have?" Brother Linus said. "Charlie, I only mentioned it because you remind me of myself. I don't know what your plans are but you seemed to come alive when we were working on the play. Acting is a rough existence and hard work. I made a very few friends whom I could trust because most of the people were cutthroat. It's the nature of the beast when you're all vying for the same roles."

"I can imagine," Charlie said, not knowing what to say.

"With respects to the chain, I overheard Brother Simon telling Father Mark how you lost your mother's locket and about the crucifix he was going to give you. I figured you could use a sturdy chain."

"Yeah, I can," Charlie laughed a little. "Thank you so much."

"Well, you are welcome. And whatever you decide to do with your life, I wish you only the best. Now, let's get back inside before I freeze to death," Brother Linus said and chuckled.

THE LOCKET

An icy draft blew through the cracks in the walls of the old cabin. Charlie wrapped his arms around himself while he stood by the fireplace.

"I can't believe we can't light a fire," Charlie said. "I mean, it's freezing in here."

"I know, but we can't, or the brothers will find out we're down here," Howard said. "Come on, sit down."

"Fine," Charlie said.

"I still can't believe it. That crazy old lady stole the wrong locket," Howard said and almost laughed.

"Yeah," Charlie said. "But she meant well."

"Do you think she knew it wasn't yours?"

"No, she wouldn't have put my name on the envelope if she knew."

"Oh, yeah," Howard said.

The two boys took turns trying to blow a cloud ring with their breath while they sat across the table from each other.

"I think it only works with smoking," Charlie said. "At least that's what I've seen in the movies. I've never known anyone who could actually do it."

"Maybe you're right," Howard agreed. "I'm so glad

Walters doesn't come down here."

"It's only because it's freezing."

"Another reason not to build a fire," Howard said with a laugh.

"I can't believe the school year is nearly half over," Charlie said and stood up. He started pacing while he rubbed the sleeves of his blazer. "What I wouldn't give for one of those capes the monks wear right about now. They look warm."

"Yeah, Brother Gregory told me they were made of wool." Howard joined Charlie, pacing back and forth on the opposite side of the room. "Have you met with your counselor yet?"

"I have an appointment with him in a couple weeks."

"I saw mine before the holidays. He's going to try to talk you into getting an apartment lined up and a job for after graduation. Don't let him. We're going to hit the road, remember?"

"Yeah, about that. A road trip sounds wonderful, but I'm still not sure I want to find my parents."

"You're not still angry with them, are you?"

"I don't know how I feel," Charlie said. "But even if I wanted to find them, I wouldn't know where to begin."

"Well, we don't have to. We could just drive and see where the road takes us. Maybe see how many states we could visit?"

"Sounds like an adventure."

"Exactly."

"There's just one thing. Where are we going to get a car?"

"Leave that to me," Howard said, sounding confident and looking a bit cocky.

"Then, what about money?"

"I've got some savings, and you have that box."

Charlie shook his head. "I'm not touching that. They wanted nothing to do with me so I don't want their money."

"Charlie, don't be ridiculous. They left that for you to

use."

"I know, but it would feel like.... I don't know." Charlie shook his head and stopped pacing.

Howard heard the pain in Charlie's tone even if Charlie refused to admit it. "Say, we don't have to take a road trip. We could get a place together?"

Charlie smiled. "That would be cool."

The sound of someone crunching through the snow outside caused both boys to rush to the window.

"Crap, it's Walters," Howard said.

"I thought you said he doesn't want to come here because of the cold?"

"That's what he said."

Rick stomped his feet on the porch. Howard quickly leaned against the door, holding it shut. Rick tried to open it. When it would not budge, he banged his fist against the door. "I know you're in there. Open the door, Miller," he shouted.

Charlie silently mimed for Howard to let Rick in but Howard responded with a violent shaking of his head.

"Come on you morons, it's freezing out here."

"Howard," Charlie said and tightened his jaw.

"Fine," Howard said and moved out of the way.

The door flew open and Rick stumbled in, catching himself with the table. Charlie grabbed the door and quickly closed it.

"It's about time," Rick sneered and turned around to face his two supposed friends. "What's the big idea, Miller?"

"Just messin' with ya," he answered and sauntered across the room to his chair at the table.

"Well, you're not funny," Rick spat and shivered. "How can you guys stand it in here? It's as cold as a freezer."

"No one said you have to stay," Howard said.

"What's up?" Charlie asked.

"Father Mark wants to see you, Charlie."

"Me? Why?"

"Oh, I couldn't possibly break a confidence," Rick

answered in a mocking tone. "How the hell should I know? He just told me to find you and give you the message."

"Where is he?"

"His office, duh."

"Fine," Charlie said. "Howard, you coming?"

Howard jumped up. "I'm outta here. Be sure to lock up before you leave, princess," he said and patted Rick's cold cheek.

"I'm coming with you guys," Rick shouted, following them out the door. He pulled the door closed and made sure it was secure.

When the boys reached the first floor, Father Mark was in the hallway outside his office talking with a man dressed in a long, tan wool overcoat. As they drew nearer, Charlie recognized the man was from The Towers. Before he could get a better look at his face, the man turned away and left.

"Mister MacCready, a word," Father Mark said when he noticed the boys coming down the hall.

"Yes, Father," Charlie answered, and entered the dean's office.

"You two should go find somewhere else to loiter. I don't want to see either of you when I open this door again. Is that understood?" Father Mark said.

"Yes, Father," Howard and Rick answered.

Father Mark waited for the boys to leave before he closed the door. "Please have a seat."

Charlie sat down in the chair that was in front of the large desk. He looked around the office while he tried to calm his nervousness. Father Mark's office was similar to Abbot Ambrose's. A floor to ceiling bookcase spanned the wall between the foyer and the office. There weren't as many books on it as there were on the Abbot's. Instead, there were a few potted plants, vines that hung down to the shelf below. Also, there were some old trophies used as bookends. Behind the desk was a window that overlooked the Great Lawn. Father Mark sat down in his chair.

"You wanted to see me?" Charlie said, still shivering away the cold and trying to rush things along. If he was in trouble, he wanted to get it over with as soon as possible.

Father Mark picked up an envelope.

"Brother Simon told me you talked with a Mrs. Walker after the concert at The Towers."

"Yes," Charlie said when Father Mark paused. "She said she knows my grandma."

"I see," Father Mark cocked his head and looked at Charlie. "I heard you lost your locket the day of the concert."

"Yes, I did."

"Is this it?" Father Mark emptied the contents of the envelope into his hand and held it out for Charlie to see.

"That's it! Where did you find it?"

"I didn't," Father Mark said. He closed his fingers around the locket and withdrew his hand. "The gentleman who was just here is the property manager from The Towers. He said that he had received several complaints from residents about things going missing. The common denominator was this Mrs. Walker." He paused and his expression softened. "It appears that she's a bit of a kleptomaniac."

"A what?" Charlie asked.

"She steals things."

"Oh," Charlie gasped. "She was right."

Father Mark's eyebrows raised. "Who was right?"

"Mrs. Iverson," Charlie answered. "She told me that Mrs. Walker was wearing my locket."

"Interesting," Father Mark said. He opened his hand again and looked at the small, tarnished silver locket.

"How did they find it?"

"As I said, the managers received a lot of complaints from other residents that some of their things had gone missing, expensive things, jewelry mainly. Since they all mentioned noticing it after Mrs. Walker had been to their apartments, their security did a search of Mrs. Walker's apartment. They found the stolen objects. The police were called and she could now be facing legal action."

"Wow," Charlie said.

"Another resident, a Mr. Nottingham, noticed the locket and remembered it was the one you showed them after the concert. Why on earth would you do such a thing?"

"Mrs. Walker said she knew my grandma and that my grandma had told her about the Saint Christopher medal she gave me. Mrs. Walker asked to see it. I didn't see any harm. The locket was on the same chain as the medal."

"I see," Father Mark said with a sigh.

"So, will the police need my locket for evidence?"

"No. The residents decided not to press charges as long as their belongings were returned."

"What will happen to Mrs. Walker?"

"She is moving out. I don't know where." Father Mark reached into the top drawer of his desk. He took out another padded envelope. "You remember this locket that Mrs. Iverson gave you?" he asked, showing it to Charlie.

"Yes," he answered. "I told Brother Simon it wasn't mine, and gave it back to him."

"Well, did you look inside?"

"No," Charlie answered.

Father Mark gently pried the locket open to reveal two small, faded portraits. He looked at them before showing them to Charlie. "When Brother Simon returned the locket, I took it to the manager of The Towers. He said this locket belonged to Mrs. Iverson. The photographs are of her and her husband. I think she wanted you to have it as a keepsake from her. She didn't mean it was your locket, the one you lost."

Charlie did not know what to say. He had assumed she thought the locket was his. Now, he felt awful rejecting it. "But what about her son? Shouldn't it go to him?"

"I don't think so. When I told him how I came to have it, he insisted I give it back to you saying it's what she wanted."

Charlie stared at the locket, remembering the dear elderly woman and feeling guilty for thinking she was a bit crazy.

"So, both of these are yours," Father Mark said, handing the lockets to Charlie. "Might I suggest that, in the future, you don't go passing around your treasures."

Charlie closed his fingers around the lockets and squeezed. "Yes, Father."

"Another thing, you might want to see Brother Eligius about fixing that bale on your mother's locket before you try wearing it again."

Charlie looked closer at the locket. The tiny ring that held the locket to the chain appeared to be broken. He looked back at Father Mark and nodded. "I will," he said.

"That's all I have," Father Mark said. "You may go now."

"Thank you, Father Mark," Charlie said, and made his exit.

The hallway was deserted. Charlie headed toward the stairs, thinking that Howard would be in his dorm. When he turned the corner at the end of the hall he bumped into his friend and let out a startled gasp.

"Don't do that!" he said and punched Howard on the shoulder. "You could have given me a heart attack."

They both laughed. Howard rubbed his shoulder.

"I wasn't about to go away and leave you there," Howard said. "So, I waited for you here."

"Well good. You saved me a trip upstairs."

"So, what'd Father Mark have to say?"

"The manager at The Towers found my missing locket," Charlie opened his fist to reveal the two lockets.

"Two of them?" Howard said, sounding confused.

"This one is my real locket. The other belonged to Mrs. Iverson. It was hers and she wanted me to have it. I thought she meant it was my locket, but...."

"That's really strange," Howard said. "You'd think she'd want to give it to someone in her family."

"Yeah, that's what I said, but Father Mark said her son

told him to give it to me. Guess he didn't want it."

"Buy why would she give it to you?"

"I don't know. Maybe she knew she was going to die and wanted me to have something to remember her by. Seems her family was like mine, they wanted nothing to do with her either."

"Maybe so, but it's still weird." Howard said. "Say, I have an idea. Come with me."

Howard led Charlie across the hall to the kitchen door. He pushed it open and marched inside. Charlie followed, but at a humbler pace.

Sister Margaret Mary was busy in the bakery room again, kneading a large mound of dough. She smiled when she saw the boys enter the kitchen. "With what can I help you boys?" she called while she kept kneading.

"Charlie, here, needs a little cheering up," Howard said, elbowing Charlie who was standing beside him. "An old friend of his passed away."

Sister Margaret Mary stopped kneading and gave Charlie a sympathetic look. "Oh, really? I'm so sorry."

"It's okay, I only knew her for a month," Charlie said.

Sister Margaret Mary looked at Howard, confused. "I thought you said an old friend?"

"She was old and she was a friend," Howard said, stressing the word "old."

"Oh, I see," she said with a nod, and began to knead again. "Go ahead and have Sister Faith help you. Tell her I said it's okay." She winked at them as they turned away.

Sister Faith was standing in front of the large, wooden prep table that sat in the center of the kitchen. Behind it was a large commercial gas cooktop with more burners than Charlie had patience to count at the moment. Beside it was an equally large griddle and beyond it, two large ovens. On the wall at the end of the table was a metal door that led to the walk-in freezer. To their left was the dishwashing area with sinks and a large dishwasher complete with a conveyor belt.

Sister Faith stopped chopping carrots when she saw the boys. She wiped her hands on the towel that hung from the ties of her white apron. "Master Miller, it's good to see you," she said with a smile. "And Master MacCready, you, too."

"Hi, Sister Faith," Charlie said quietly.

"What can I do for you boys?"

"Charlie here is in need of some cheering up," Howard said.

"Really? Why is that?"

"Oh, a friend of his died awhile back and she left him her locket," Howard said and turned toward Charlie. "Show it to her."

Charlie held out the tarnished silver locket.

"What a beautiful trinket," Sister Faith said. "She must have thought a lot of you to give you such a precious gift."

"That's what I told him, but he's too broken up about it to listen."

Charlie looked at Howard. He could not believe the con job he was playing on Sister Faith.

"Well, in that case, I suppose that means a slice of apple pie?"

"And ice cream," Howard added. "If it's not too much trouble, I mean."

"Of course, it wouldn't be the same without it," she answered and winked at Charlie. She took a pie from one of the racks on wheels that sat near the ovens and set it on the table. "Grab a couple dessert plates and forks," she told Howard. When he returned with them, she continued, "You know where the ice cream is."

"I sure do," Howard said and disappeared into the walk-in freezer.

"I suppose this is more of Master Miller's idea than yours?" she whispered to Charlie when they were alone.

Charlie nodded. "Yes, Sister."

"I see. Did you really get some bad news?" she asked while she cut two big slices of freshly baked apple pie and put them on the plates.

"Yes. Mrs. Iverson, my friend at The Towers, died a week before Christmas break."

Sister Faith froze and looked at him. "I'm so sorry," she said. Her blue eyes cast him a concerned, sympathetic look.

"It's okay, I mean, I'm okay," Charlie said.

"I'm sure you are, but it's okay to feel sad."

Charlie bit his lower lip and looked away. Her gentle, motherly words tugged at his heart and stirred up his emotions. He turned his head away because he did not want to cry in front of her, again. Luckily, Howard emerged from the freezer with a large round tub in his hands. He kicked the freezer door closed and quickly set the tub on the end of the table by Sister Faith.

"Oh, would you grab the scoop from the drawer over there," she said, nodding in the direction of the cupboards by the sink.

"Sure," Howard said. He quickly retrieved the item and handed it to Sister Faith.

Both boys watched as she dug the scoop deep into the ice cream and pulled it out. She placed an extra-large ball of ice cream on each plate before putting the lid back on the tub. She handed the ice cream scoop to Howard and asked him to put it in the sink for her while she returned the ice cream to the freezer.

"You boys can pull a stool out from under the table and have a seat here," she called over her shoulder.

"Thank you, Sister," Howard answered. He pulled the plates across the table and set one in front of Charlie and the other in front of him. Before he sat down, he took a bite. "Oh, my," he said. "This pie is delicious."

Sister Faith laughed at the compliment, seeing how Howard was overacting. She grabbed the ladle and stirred the large pot of stew. She added the carrots before moving on to the next pot.

When the boys were finished, Sister Faith told Howard to put their plates in the sink.

"I trust everything was satisfactory?"

"Oh, yes," Howard said, putting his hand on his flat stomach. "That hit the spot."

"How about you, Master MacCready? Was it okay?" she asked.

"More than okay, Sister Faith," he answered. "Thank you so much."

"My pleasure," she said. "Well, I need to be minding the stew so it doesn't burn." She tilted her head toward the door.

"We should go, then," Howard said and jumped to his feet. He slid his stool back under the table. Charlie did the same. "See you tonight at dinner," Howard said as the two left the kitchen.

"She sure is nice," Howard said once they were back in the main hallway.

"She is. Did I ever tell you that she has the same name as my mom?"

"I think you wrote me about it last year," Howard said. He stopped suddenly and grabbed Charlie's arm. "Say, have you ever wondered if your parents could be watching you now?"

Charlie's eyebrows pinched above his nose. "Why would you say that?"

"I don't know, it was just a thought. Sister Faith and your mom's name is Faith. The way Father Mark calls you son."

"But so does Abbot Ambrose and Father Cecil. That doesn't mean anything."

"Are you sure?" Howard said, turning his head to the side but keeping his eyes on Charlie. "It might be a starting point."

"Nah, that's crazy," Charlie said, shaking his head.

"I wouldn't be too quick to dismiss the idea." Howard yawned loudly. "I don't know about you, but I could sure use a nap."

Charlie remembered the locket. "You go on and I'll catch you later. I've got something to do."

"Okay, see you later," Howard said and headed up the stairs.

Charlie continued down the main hall to the foyer door. He walked across the room to the large wooden double doors of the monastery wing. He opened the one on the right and entered.

A brother sitting behind the reception desk looked up when he approached. "May I help you?" he asked.

"Is Brother, uh," Charlie had forgotten the name Father Mark said. He looked at the locket in his hand. "Is the brother who fixes broken lockets busy?"

The receptionist looked at the locket and smiled. "You mean Brother Eligius. Let me check." He picked up the receiver from his telephone and dialed a four-digit number. Turning his back on Charlie, he spoke into the phone. When he turned back around, he put the receiver back on its base. "He will be right down. Go ahead and have a seat over there." The brother directed Charlie to the chairs against the wall by the doors.

The clock on the wall above him loudly ticked away the minutes. It felt like forever before Charlie heard the sound of footsteps coming closer. He looked at the hallway behind the reception desk. A short, stubby, bald monk wearing his glasses on top of his head like a tiara waddled closer. Charlie stood up. The monk stopped at the reception desk and spoke to the brother. The bald monk glanced at Charlie and nodded, then turned around and headed back the way he came.

"Was that him?" Charlie asked.

The foyer door opened and another monk entered. The brother was slightly shorter than Charlie. He had dark hair with a slight reddish tint. His eyes were brown. He walked straight over to Charlie.

"Hello, Master MacCready," he said in a deep voice and held out his hand.

Charlie stood up and shook the brother's hand.

"I understand you need some help with a locket?" Brother Eligius said, sounding uncertain.

"Yes, Father Mark said I should have you look at it and maybe fix it."

"Let me see," he said.

"Father Mark said something about a bale?" Charlie said while he took the locket from the pocket of his slacks. He held it out to Brother Eligius. Charlie thought he saw the monk smile faintly when he opened the locket, but he was not sure.

Brother Eligius held it up to the light. He nodded his head. "I think I can do something. Would you like to come and watch?" he said.

"Sure, if you don't mind," Charlie answered. "I let it out of my sight once and nearly lost it for good."

Brother Eligius gave Charlie a look of shock but quickly smiled. "No problem. Come along to my workshop."

The monk led Charlie around the reception desk and down the hall of the monastery wing. He turned left at the end and headed down the side hallway that led toward the back of the abbey. At the last door on the left, he stopped. Reaching into his pocket, he took out a key. "It's the only door in this part of the abbey that has a lock," he said as he opened the door.

Charlie followed the brother inside. The room was a little larger than Father Cecil's cell, or at least it seemed that way. The curtainless window that overlooked the monks' cloistered garden let in enough light to fill the room. A glass display counter like those in the museum divided the room in half. Behind it, beneath the window, was a workbench that spanned the width of the room. On its wooden countertop were scattered various tools. A ring light with a large magnifying glass center was affixed to a mechanical arm and bolted to the countertop. On either side of the window, hugging the walls, was a wide but shallow case with several small drawers, each with a white label but Charlie could not make out what was on them.

Brother Eligius walked around the end of the display case to his workbench. Charlie stepped up to the case and looked down. Inside, on the black velvet bottom of the shallow display, were watches of all sorts, pocket, wrist, even a pendant watch on a retractable pin like Sister Faith's. There were also rings, some with gemstones, others plain gold bands. Charlie thought it odd that there would be such expensive looking jewelry in a monastery where the residents took a vow of poverty.

"Admiring the jewelry?" Brother Eligius asked.

Charlie jumped and looked at the monk. "Oh, yeah, I guess."

Brother Eligius stepped closer to the case. "We receive a lot of donations in the form of jewelry. Usually as part of a bequest after the owner passes away. I clean it up, and some of it we sell in our gift shop. Other pieces, we melt down the gold to make other things. Take this one," he said and opened the back of the case. He took out a gold chain with a pendent. "The owner brought in her wedding ring after her husband divorced her. She had me melt it down and make this out of it. The diamond that dots the I was the diamond from her ring."

"What's it say?"

"*Ciao*. It's Italian for goodbye."

"Oh," Charlie said.

"Sad thing, she never came back for it. Perhaps she found a new love and moved on?" He put the necklace back in the case. "Now, it won't take long for me to fix the bale on your locket, so feel free to browse." His smile was kind. He turned his back to his workbench. "So, where did you get such a beautiful piece of jewelry?"

"My grandmother gave it to me a long time ago. It was my mother's."

There was the sound of something hitting the floor. Brother Eligius quickly retrieved the pair of tiny pliers. "I'm sorry, you were saying?"

"My grandmother gave it to me. Inside is a picture of my parents," he said.

"Oh, that's who they are," the monk said and bobbed his head. "They're a nice-looking couple."

"I suppose," Charlie said.

"Suppose? What an odd thing to say."

"Well, I don't really remember them. In fact, I don't think I would know them if I saw them."

"Why's that?"

"I was only two years old when they left me with my grandmother."

"Left you. What happened to them?"

"I don't know. I think they are either dead or in hiding from someone."

"Really? How strange. Has anyone tried to find them?"

"My grandma said the police tried, but that was fifteen years ago. My friend Howard wants us to take a road trip after graduation in May to see if we can find them, but I'm not sure I want to."

"Why's that?"

"My grandma told me when my mom dropped me off that she would return for me. For years I wanted to believe it, but she never came back. I don't think they really wanted me and now, I don't want them."

"Oh, my," Brother Eligius said, turning back around. "I don't think she doesn't want you."

"Then, they must be dead," Charlie said. "Rick says I need to face the facts and move on."

"Rick?"

"He's another friend of mine."

"Well, he sounds a bit harsh." Brother Eligius tilted his head and looked at Charlie with sad, empathetic eyes. "I'm sure there is a logical explanation. Maybe something you haven't thought of yet."

"Yeah, you know what Howard just said?" Charlie realized how stupid that sounded and quickly went on. "He said maybe my parents are already here and watching me."

Brother Eligius let out a choked laugh. "How could they hide?"

"Since I have no idea what they look like, I suppose they could be pretending to be a monk and a nun."

The jeweler shook his head. "I seriously doubt Abbot Ambrose would go along with that." He placed the locket on the glass countertop. "There you go, good or even better than new."

Charlie looked at the locket. The small ring bale was whole again. The whole locket seemed to shine and sparkle more, too.

"Wow," he said.

"I polished it up a bit. Removed some of that tarnish. It could use a bit more cleaning to really sparkle."

"No, it looks great. How much do I owe you?"

Brother Eligius huffed and shook his head. "Nothing. I do it all the time. It's my pleasure."

"Are you sure?" Charlie asked still marveling at how fast the work had gone and how beautiful the locket appeared.

"Yes, I am," he answered.

"Well, thank you so much." Charlie quickly took the gold chain around his neck. The key and the medal hit each other and made a soft tink sound. Charlie thought he heard Brother Eligius gasp but he was not sure. He opened the clasp and slipped the chain through the new bale. He fastened it again and put the chain around his neck. "Thank you again," he said and started for the door.

"Charlie." Brother Eligius stopped him.

"Yes, Brother," Charlie said, and turned back around. He noticed the expression on Brother Eligius's face. It was as if he was worried about something.

"Have a good day," he said, and smiled.

"You, too," Charlie said and left the workshop.

THE UNWANTED BOY

The sun felt warm against Charlie's cheeks but the air in the shade was still cold. Winter was teasing him, pretending to be spring. Charlie looked at the pond while he sat beside Father Cecil. The goldfish were swimming near the surface, where the water was warmer. Charlie watched them but was not really seeing them. His mind was elsewhere.

"Penny for your thoughts," Father Cecil said, breaking the silence.

"I'm just thinking," Charlie said.

"About?"

"About something Abbot Ambrose told us resident boys the other day. He said that after graduation, if we decide to leave, the abbey would help get us started with getting us an apartment and a job. Why would they do that? How can they do that?"

"It's what any parent would do for their young adult child. Since the resident boys still here have no parents to rely on for that needed support, the abbey provides it. Our door is always open, should any of you need us."

"Oh," Charlie said. "I see."

"Is that all that's on your mind?"

"No."

"You know you can tell me anything, son."

"That's just it," Charlie said. "Why do you call me son?"

Father Cecil shrugged his shoulders. "I don't know. It's just an endearing term. I mean, for a priest who doesn't have actual children of his own, the flock that he shepherds are like his children. Does it bother you?"

"No. No," Charlie answered. "It's just something Howard said a while ago. He said what if my parents were here but hiding, pretending to be a monk or like Sister Faith in the kitchen."

"Like Sister Faith? You don't believe she's a nun?"

"No, it's not that." Charlie shook his head and felt confused. "My mother's name was Faith. I know it sounds dumb, but I can't get Howard's idea out of my head and it's making me crazy. I find myself looking at each monk and wondering if he's really my dad."

"Oh, son, I wish I knew how to help you. I honestly am at a loss for words."

"It's okay. I know I'm just being stupid," Charlie said, and looked down at the pond again. "Just don't let him be Father Vicar." Father Cecil laughed out loud which made Charlie do the same.

"I can assure you," Father Cecil said. "Vicar is not your father. He came to the abbey, much like you, abandoned by his mother but he was left on the doorstep when he was a baby."

"Why?" Charlie asked, surprised by this new revelation.

"His mother was a young unwed girl. Very Catholic. She knew she couldn't raise the child. In those days, it was unheard of. So, once he was born, she left him here."

"Does Father Vicar know? Is that what made him so mean?"

"No. Vicar was a sensitive boy and small for his age. The other boys teased and harassed him something awful. He didn't reach a growth spurt until he was well into his teens. By then his tormentors were gone."

"So, that's why he hates children?"

"He doesn't hate children, son. He hates what he perceives as weakness because other children, like birds in the wild, will peck at a bird that is weak."

"But, why does he dislike me?"

"I think you remind him of himself."

"No way," Charlie said.

"It's true. When you arrived here, you were shorter than most of the boys in your class."

"I wasn't the shortest," Charlie protested.

"But you weren't among the taller ones," Father Cecil continued. "Add to that, you wouldn't speak. That was something other boys would see as a challenge. Then, when they found out your history, it made you vulnerable. You yourself said that Dougary and his—Oh, what did you call them?—goons tormented you and your friends."

"Yes," Charlie said. Father Cecil's words were beginning to sink in.

"Vicar wanted you to toughen up. Albeit, he went about it in the wrong way but his heart was in the right place."

Charlie was silent. This was a completely different image of the school principal that was forming in his mind. Instead of a sinister, sadistic priest, the image of a bullied and misunderstood boy who did not want to see others be mistreated took shape. He now understood why Father Vicar always stood so straight, with his chin raised.

"Tell me, Father," Charlie said. "Did he ever meet his mother?"

Father Cecil shook his head. "No, not when he was a child, but she did come to see him several times after he joined the Order but he refused to see her. She wrote him letters but, according to him, he sent them back unopened. The last time she came here was on the day of his ordination, but he would not even acknowledge her. She passed away a year later."

"How sad," Charlie said. He thought about his parents and how he said he would ignore them if they came. "So, is that why he never laughs or smiles?"

"He's the only one who can answer that."

Charlie looked at the pond. He felt bad for Father Vicar and understood how he must have felt. Charlie then began to wonder if he would turn out the same—a bitter, mean man.

"So, are you thinking of leaving us?" Father Cecil said.

"I'm not sure," Charlie answered. "Howard said we should get an apartment together."

"That might be fun."

"I suppose."

"With the money your parents left you, you wouldn't struggle to make ends meet."

"I'm not touching it. I don't want it."

Father Cecil heard the bitterness in Charlie's voice. He gave Charlie's knee a pat. "It's okay."

They sat in silence for a while, soaking up the warmth from the sun. Charlie looked across the Great Lawn at the gymnasium when he heard someone talking. Father Cecil heard it, too, and turned his face in the direction.

"What's that about?" he asked.

"It's just some guys going to tryouts for the spring play," he said.

"Oh? Why aren't you trying out? I heard you made a great ghost in the last play."

"This one's going to be a musical. You have to be a good singer and I'm not."

"Really? I'd have thought being in the choir would make you a good candidate."

"Yeah, singing with other people is one thing, but not alone," Charlie said. Already, just talking about it, awakened his nerves and made him feel a bit nauseous. "No, it's not for me."

"Okay," Father Cecil said and nodded. "So, what are your plans for the rest of the year?"

"The year?"

"The school year."

"I don't know," Charlie said. "Go to classes and stuff. What else is there?"

"I don't mean to tell you what to do, but you really should think about your future. I understand if you want to go on to college somewhere, you have to submit your application soon."

"That's what Rick says, too. I just don't know. I guess I expected things to be different by now. I mean...."

"I know, but it's time to put all of that aside and take charge of your own life. Have you ever thought about becoming a policeman or a detective?"

"No. Why would you think of that?"

Father Cecil laughed. "I was thinking about how you solved the mystery of the locket, the note, and the key. That was pretty good work."

"Dumb luck, is more like it," he said. "I really didn't solve anything."

"Modesty," Father Cecil said, bobbing his head slightly.

"I have thought about becoming a teacher."

"What subject?"

"I was thinking maybe English. I like to write. Did I tell you my grandma sent me a journal to write in?"

"Yes. Have you been?"

"A couple times. She said to write about special moments. Stuff like that. So, that's what I'm doing."

"I see."

"Anyway, I'm not a hundred per cent sure about teaching. It's just a thought."

"Well, it's something. For that you would need to decide on a college and fill out an application."

"I'll talk to Abbot Ambrose about it."

"Good. What time is it?"

"It's almost two."

"I should be getting back to my cell. Do you mind?"

"No, not at all."

Charlie helped Father Cecil back to the abbey. He then went to meet Howard and Gus in the cabin.

~§~

Charlie's mind was still so focused on his conversation with Father Cecil that he missed the turn for the cabin and found himself standing at the top of Black Butte amid the charred remnants of the destroyed abbey. It had been nearly two summers since he was there. Nothing had really changed. The pile of rubble where he found the cornerstone was still there. But now he noticed something different. Amid the ruins, behind the cornerstone, the marble floor of the abbey church between the skeletal walls was still intact, though badly damaged. Curiosity took over and Charlie crawled over the fallen façade.

The pews on either side of the center aisle were gone. All that was left were darkened marks in the flooring. Charlie looked up at the remnants of the walls. The heavy timbers were charred black and looked as if they would crumble with the slightest of breeze. He could see in one section where a stained-glass window once was and wondered what it had depicted. The marble altar in the sanctuary was shattered by a fallen beam. All that was left was a pile of rubble. Charlie looked all around and felt sad. This was once the home and church of the brothers. Now, because of a fire, it was gone, and everything was lost in one night.

He cautiously continued, deeper into the rubble to explore behind the sanctuary and more the ruins. Past the altar, the building was completely gone. Grass grew where once there was floor. The walls, apparently made more of wood than the stone in the church portion, were gone. Only a few charred pieces remained poking up out of the ground.

Something caught Charlie's eye. A large hole in the ground. Remembering that Abbot Ambrose had warned him the ground was unstable due to the catacombs beneath, Charlie moved more slowly.

Standing at the top of the hole, he looked at the stone steps that lead down into the darkness below. He considered exploring it, but realized without a light, he would not be able to see. Plus, he felt a bit creeped out by the thought of what he might find. Abbot Ambrose had told him the brothers relocated the coffins of those who were entombed in the catacombs to the cemetery, but did they get them all? Charlie decided against exploring on his own and headed back to the path to the cabin.

When he reached the cabin, Howard was waiting inside with Gus.

"Hi, guys," he said when he entered.

"Hi. What kept you?" Howard asked, looking up from his solitaire card game.

"I was lost in my head and missed the path. I ended up at the top of Black Butte," Charlie answered while he pulled out a chair and sat down at the table.

"Not you, too?" Howard said and played a card.

"Me, too? What do you mean?"

"He's talking about me," Gus answered. "Father Mark thinks I should take the entrance exam for college this weekend."

"Father Cecil thinks I should do the same," Charlie said, not sounding enthused. "I know Rick is going to."

"Rick has to do everything anyone else is doing," Howard said. He pulled all the cards into a pile and then shaped them back into a deck. He left them on the center of the table and sat back.

"What about you?" Charlie asked. "What does your counselor say?"

"He said I should, too. It's crazy. He's crazy. Why would I voluntarily use up a Saturday afternoon taking a stupid test?"

"It's not all afternoon," Gus said. "It's two hours."

"Exactly. Two, long, painful hours of sweating over a test to see if I'm smart enough for their stupid college."

"So, you're not taking it?" Charlie asked.

"I didn't say that. Are you?"

"Why not? It doesn't mean I'll get accepted or even go if I am. Father Cecil said it will at least give me an option."

"I guess," Howard said. "I might as well. It will get Brother Gregory off my back about it.

~§~

Saturday arrived. The clock above the chalkboard ticked loudly—at least Charlie thought he heard it. He sat at his desk, staring at the official looking test. It was not the usual mimeographed test like the ones he was used to in his classes. The ones with the intoxicating smell. This test was printed on heavy paper with a separate instruction sheet. Father Vicar read the instructions aloud while the boys followed along before the test began. When he was finished, he asked if there were any questions. Everyone looked at Rick, but Rick did not raise his hand. Father Vicar then gave his own rules. "Keep your heads down. Eyes on your own test. No talking. No noisemaking. No copying from your neighbor's test. If you have to use the restroom, do it now or else hold it until after the test. If you leave the room before finishing, your test will be thrown out. When you are finished, bring your test to me and then quietly leave the room."

Charlie did his best to comply. However, after an hour, he did steal a glance at the clock and looked at how much he had left to do on the test. There were ten pages in all and he had only completed four. At this rate he would finish two pages short. He began to rush.

A half an hour later, Rick brought his test to Father Vicar. Then another boy, and another. Charlie was beginning to feel the pressure. He did not want to be the last, yet, he did not want to fail.

Focus, Charlie, focus, the voice in his head said.

When Father Vicar called time, Charlie still had half a page to go. He handed in his test and waited for Howard and

Gus in the hallway.

"How do you think you did?" he asked them.

"I don't think I did too bad," Gus said, with a bit more confidence than Charlie had expected.

"What about you, Howard?"

"I think I did okay. Enough to get in if I want. You?"

"I think I bombed it."

"Why?" Howard asked.

"I didn't finish."

The classroom door opened and Father Vicar stood on the threshold. His back straightened and his chin raised. He held the stack of tests close to his chest. "Shouldn't you boys be finding somewhere else to be?" he said in a cold and threatening tone.

"Yes, Father," they answered and headed for the fire doors.

Once in the stairwell, Charlie looked back. He watched the principal walk into his office. Charlie remembered what Father Cecil had told him and he felt his heart soften toward the unwanted boy.

"What's the matter?" Howard asked, giving Charlie a shoulder bump.

"Oh, nothing," Charlie answered. "When are we supposed to get the results?"

"I dunno," Howard answered.

"Rick told me it takes two weeks," Gus said.

"Two weeks?" Howard exclaimed. "Why so long?"

"They send the tests to some place to be run through a machine, like they did for the SATs. I guess those people do it for all the colleges, so it takes time. What's the big deal? You're not serious about getting in anyway," Gus said.

"Maybe I am," Howard said defiantly.

"Really?" Charlie asked.

"Yeah," he answered with an uncertain head bob.

"Me, too, I guess," Charlie admitted.

"Hey, wouldn't it be neat if all of us went on to college

here? You two, Rick and me," Gus said.

"You had to throw Rick in the mix," Howard said. "You almost had me."

"It would, I mean, if I decide to stay," Charlie said.

"This is all too much thinking," Howard said. "I'm going to see if I can swipe a cookie or two. Wanna come?"

"Do you have to ask?" Gus said.

The boys headed to the kitchen.

CLOSURE

Two weeks had passed, feeling like an eternity, since the boys took their entrance exams. Charlie, Howard, and Gus sat in the back of the gymnasium not-so-quietly watching Rick rehearsing for the new musical.

"What's the name of this?" Howard asked.

"*Oliver*," Charlie answered.

"What's it about?"

"It's Charles Dickens's story, *Oliver Twist*," Charlie said.

Howard shrugged and looked unimpressed.

"The story of an orphaned boy who runs away and gets mixed up with a bunch of pickpockets," Charlie said. "We were supposed to read it our freshman year."

"Oh, yeah, the one with the mean dog, Sikes," Howard said, with a knowing nod.

"It was actually Bull's-eye," Gus corrected. "But close enough."

"Yeah, yeah," Howard said, dismissively. "So, who's Rick supposed to be in this?"

"For the umpteenth time, Fagin," Gus answered, sounding exasperated. "He's the leader of the pickpockets."

"Oh," Howard said. "I guess it fits."

Charlie and Gus both gave Howard a confused look. "Why's that?"

"His character is a creep and so is he," Howard said with a smug grin.

"You're impossible," Charlie said, rolling his eyes while he shook his head.

"You have to admit, he's pretty good," Gus said.

"If he wasn't, he wouldn't have been given the part," Howard said.

Again, Charlie was confused, but Howard was a complicated kind of friend. One minute he would put Rick down, and then next, compliment him. One constant, Charlie knew, was that Howard would defend his friends to the bitter end. He was a good guy with a kind heart.

"What time is it?" Howard asked when Rick walked off the stage.

"It's almost four," Charlie said, looking at his pocket watch. "Why?"

"I wonder if the afternoon mail has been delivered."

"You're thinking about your test results," Gus said.

"More wondering why I haven't received mine," Howard answered. "Rick got his two days ago, and has been gloating ever since."

"I got mine yesterday," Gus said.

"You did?" Charlie said, sounding surprised. "Why didn't you say anything?"

"I haven't opened it. I'm too scared. What if I failed? Then where do I go? What would I do?"

"Hey, we're buds, we'll help each other," Howard said. "What about you, Charlie?"

Charlie shook his head. "I haven't received mine either."

"I wonder why? Maybe it's because our names start with M?"

"Maybe. I don't know."

"Well, there's always our road trip," Howard said.

"Maybe. I'm still not sure I want to go looking for someone who doesn't care enough in fifteen years to try to contact me."

"Charlie, don't be like that," Gus said. "If my parents were out there somewhere, I'd do anything to find them."

"I keep looking at how the other guys' parents are when they come to pick up their sons. They always seem happy. They hug them, even though they saw them a month ago. It's like they really missed them. I keep wondering what is so horrible that my parents wouldn't want to see me?"

Howard sat up from leaning his chair against the back wall of the gym. He glanced at Gus who was seated to his left and then to Charlie, on his right. "Hey, what's this?" he said. "You know, the one thing I always liked—no, admired—about you, Charlie? You were always so sure your parents were out there and had unwavering faith that one day they'd come for you. Now, I know lately you've been disappointed because it hasn't happened yet, but, don't think for a minute they don't love you. Look at me. I thought my dad didn't want me because he put me in here, but I was wrong. So, maybe there's a good reason for them not coming forward."

Charlie looked at Howard and forced a smile. "Thanks."

"I get what's going on," Gus said. "My counselor calls it lack of closure. For me, the funeral for my parents was closure, a period at the end of the sentence. But you've never had that."

"Because they aren't dead," Charlie snapped back. His expression softened. "At least I don't think they are. Well, maybe that's why they haven't come for me?"

"What do you say we have our own little funeral for them?" Gus said.

Charlie looked confused. All the funerals he had been to always had a dead person. His parents were not dead. Still, he thought about what Gus said. Maybe he was right. Maybe they could have a mock funeral for them to give him the period at the end of the sentence. "I don't know. I'll have to think about it," he said.

~§~

Charlie stood outside Father Cecil's cell staring at the door. Gus's suggestion two days ago kept inserting itself into his thoughts when he was not thinking of anything in particular. It troubled him because he was beginning to lean toward having a mock funeral. He knocked.

The sound of Father Cecil bumping into something and his yelp penetrated the door. Charlie knew instantly that someone had visited before him and had moved something. The door opened. Father Cecil was rubbing his knee.

"Hi, Father," Charlie said.

"Ah, Master McCready," he said and grinned. "Come in. Come in." He hobbled back to his chair in the corner.

Charlie saw a chair tipped over on the floor partially hidden beneath the table. He pulled it out and righted it. Sitting down he said, "I see you had a visitor."

"Brother Linus," he said, still rubbing his knee.

"Are you okay?"

"I think so. It just smarts a bit. So, how have you been? Any news about your exam?"

"Yes," Charlie said. "I received an acceptance letter today."

Father Cecil sat back and smiled proudly. "That's wonderful, son."

"I suppose," Charlie said.

"Uh-oh, what's troubling you?"

"I keep thinking about something Gus said. That maybe we should have a funeral of sorts for my parents."

"Why would you do that?"

"For closure. If they were alive, they would have come back for me by now. Hoping for the last fifteen years has been a waste of time."

"I see," Father Cecil said, nodding his head slightly. "And you think having this memorial for them will help you move on?"

"It might," Charlie answered, but sounded less sure. "I mean...I don't know. Gus seems to think it will. He said having a funeral helped him when his parents died. It was sort of final. He couldn't pretend it didn't happen. They were dead."

"So do you intend on having a Funeral Mass?"

"No, I was thinking we could just have a prayer and sort of say goodbye to them that way."

"Who is this we?"

"Just Howard and Gus, so far. Rick's too busy with the play."

"But, son, you've said all along that your parents are alive."

"I know. I don't know what to do. I just feel so lost," Charlie said.

"I can understand that. Have you talked about this with your counselor, Abbot Ambrose?"

"No," Charlie said.

"Perhaps you should. He's a wise man."

"Maybe I will," Charlie said, sounding depressed.

"Well, think about it a bit more, at least. So, how are your classes going?"

"Great," Charlie's tone perked up. "This final quarter, I don't have as many classes because I've already earned enough credits to graduate."

"Wonderful."

"I can't believe in eight weeks I'll be receiving my diploma. My grandma has already arranged for my cap and gown. She's looking forward to coming. I think my Aunt Bernice is bringing her." Charlie's smile faded. "I wish my parents could see me graduate."

"I know, son," Father Cecil said. "But, remember those of us who are there dearly love you and are proud of you."

"I will try," Charlie said, and smiled.

EASTER

Charlie quietly closed the door as he left Abbot Ambrose's office. His conversation with his great-uncle ran longer than he had anticipated. All of the other boys would already be in bed and the lights out. Quietly, he made his way up the stairs. His thoughts were still on his conversation and the abbot's advice.

As expected, the dormitory was dark. Not even the moonlight shining in seemed to dispel it. Charlie stood by the doors and waited for his eyes to adjust to the darkness. He skipped going to his locker to change clothes. Instead, he carefully made his way to his cubicle. He took off his clothes and crawled into bed in his underwear. It would have to do for the night.

The next morning, Gus bumped into the partition when he climbed out of bed. The loud bang startled Charlie from his sleep. He sat up and waited for the fog of slumber to clear from his head before he threw the covers off.

After he showered, he returned to his locker. Howard was dressed and waiting for him.

"Where were you last night? You just disappeared."

"I was talking to Abbot Ambrose."

"Must have been some talk. Where did you go after that?"

"To bed. It was late. After lights out."

"Good grief, what—" Howard stopped himself. A sad expression came over his face. "Is your grandma okay?"

Charlie's eyebrows pinched together. "Of course, she is. Why would you think that?"

"I don't know, maybe because you were gone all evening. I thought it must be serious."

"Well, it kind of was," Charlie said.

"Well, spill it. What did you guys talk about?"

"Stuff," Charlie answered and waved Howard off with a shaking of his head.

"Oh, I get it," Howard said knowingly. "Your parents. Hey, if you don't want to go looking for them, we don't have to. We could just hang out at my dad's until we come back in the fall."

"You're actually going to come back for college?"

"Yes, and don't look so surprised," Howard said. "It's the only college I applied for and tested for. I guess I was still hoping you'd change your mind about the road trip idea."

"Yeah, sorry about that. But we could take a trip to the beach or someplace."

"Okay, that could be fun," Howard said. His smile faded. "So, did you talk about the mock funeral idea with him?"

"I mentioned it."

"And...."

"He nixed it. He said it's too premature to bury them. I told him I don't care anymore, to me they may as well be dead. They don't want anything to do with me, so why should I hold out hope that they will come back."

"Wow, what did he say to that?"

"Not much. But he did insist that I not give up on them entirely."

"Do you think he knows more than he's letting on? After all, he knew about everything else, the key, the box, your dad's parents, and all that."

"I don't know. If he does, he does. I'm tired of playing games, and being told to wait until I'm grown up," Charlie said as he tucked his shirttails into his pants. "As I said, I'm done. Time to move on, like everyone keeps telling me."

"I'm really sorry," Howard said.

"Don't be. Hey, a month from now we'll have graduated."

"Yeah!" Howard said, then became pensive. "I'm gonna miss this floor." He looked at the cubicles and lounge while Charlie took his shoes and socks back to his cubicle to put them on. "Say, can't I get you to change your mind about coming home with me for Easter? My dad is going to make a glazed ham and we're going to rent some movies, have a guys' weekend."

"I can't. I told Brother Gregory I'd help out with the Easter egg hunt."

"I thought the monks handled that? They always did in the past."

"Yeah, well, with only six of us resident boys, he wants us to get more involved and not sit around all day. Besides, I can't leave Gus alone."

"I thought he was going home with Rick?"

"He told me Rick's mom changed her mind. Something about Rick's dad being there and her wanting it to be a family holiday."

"Really? Are they getting back together?"

"Who knows?" Charlie said, and stood.

"Speaking of Walters, tonight's the opening night for his play. You going?"

"Yep. I want to see how he does."

"I'm surprised there are only three shows for this one. You know there aren't any shows on Sunday?"

"Yes. I half expected it to be the same as the Christmas play. Oh well, it doesn't really matter because I'm not in it. Hey, we better get to morning prayer."

~§~

That evening, Charlie, Howard, and Gus quietly took their seats in the center of the last row of chairs on the main floor of the gymnasium. The velvet stage curtains looked amazing to Charlie. He had only seen them from the other side. In rehearsals, Brother Linus had the stagehands use only the inner curtains. Charlie felt his anticipation for the play to start grow.

"So, how do you think he'll do?" Howard asked, leaning closer to Charlie and whispering.

"He should do great. God knows he's been practicing enough. He really shouldn't sing about picking pockets while he's showering."

"True. That was a little creepy showering in the stall next to his," Howard said. "When I see someone rich, all my fingers start to twitch," Howard crooned and all three boys laughed.

"Some crowd," Gus said, looking at the chairs filling up in front of them. "You know what would make this even better?"

"Popcorn," Charlie and Howard said together and then broke into laughter again.

"Yes," Gus said. "I don't know why they don't let us have any food or something to drink."

"Because, if you spill anything on the canvas tarps covering the floor, it will leave a mark on the tarp. Plus, if everyone spilled their drinks, it could soak through and ruin the hardwood floor beneath," Howard said, mimicking Brother Linus's voice.

"They let us have refreshments at other times," Gus protested.

"I know, but that's what Brother Linus said," Howard agreed.

The school's orchestra began playing. The audience

quieted down to listen. The lights began to dim and the velvet curtain raised while the inner curtains parted. Charlie felt the excitement in the air. The lights on the stage brightened, and the play began.

Charlie was in awe of the sets. They looked amazing, as if there really were a dungeon, a seedy London street, a glorious palace right there on the stage. Even the acting and singing were magical. Charlie applauded until his hands burned. Even Howard was impressed. He whistled sharply as he clapped.

"That was awesome," Gus said while the three made their way out of the gym. They huddled together at the edge of the patio by one of the large planter boxes.

"Walters wasn't bad," Howard said.

"I thought he did a really good job," Charlie said.

"How long do you think it will take him to change?" Gus asked.

"Not long. When he played Bob Cratchit, he got changed really fast. But it took a little more makeup this time to turn him into a dirty street bum," Charlie said.

"It was a good look for him," Howard teased.

"I still think they should let us have popcorn," Gus said.

"Give it a rest," Howard told him. "You've been harping on that all through the play. It's over."

"Well, I'm gonna sneak in some candy next time."

"Don't get caught. They'll throw you out and you'll get work crew."

"Ooo," Gus mocked. "School's almost over. Who cares?"

"You will if you have to clean toilets all day for a week," Howard said.

"I won't get caught," Gus said defiantly.

"Hey, there he is," Charlie said and stood up. "Rick, over here!" He waved his hand in the air.

Rick looked at them and reluctantly walked over to them.

"Hey, why do you look so glum?" Howard asked,

seeing Rick's expression.

"Don't pretend you didn't notice," Rick said.

"Notice what?"

"Yeah, what?" Howard agreed with Charlie.

"My second scene, I flubbed my lines."

"You did?" Gus said, sounding surprised.

"Yes," Rick said. "After the scene, I told Brother Linus I can't go back on stage. I can't. I'm too embarrassed."

"What did he say?"

"First he slapped me and told me to pull myself together. Then he told me I was going to go back out there and finish what I started."

"He slapped you? Can he do that?" Gus asked.

"He did," Rick said.

"God, I wish I could have seen that," Howard said with a huge grin.

Rick glared at him. "Not funny, Miller."

"Rick, I didn't notice, and I'm sure none of the rest of the audience did either. Unless they have a script, no one could tell. You did great and should be proud of that," Charlie said.

"You sound like Brother Linus," Rick said.

"Well, put it out of your mind. You were wonderful."

"Yeah, for as much as I love to tease you, you did good, Walters. I didn't even notice your screw up." Howard said.

"Really?" Rick's sad expression began to brighten.

"Yes. You know me, I wouldn't compliment you for anything. So, knock 'em dead the next time."

"It's 'break a leg'," Rick corrected.

"Don't tempt me."

The four boys laughed as they headed across the Great Lawn to the abbey.

~§~

The week before Easter passed quickly. The students had left at noon on Friday to spend the holiday week at home with their families. Howard tried one last time to change Charlie's mind about staying behind, but to no avail. Instead, they said their goodbyes, and Charlie watched as Howard and his father drove away.

Saturday left no time for Charlie to think about what he was missing with Howard. He helped the brothers tidy up the flower beds dotting the Great Lawn.

"Aren't we supposed to mow the grass?" Charlie asked.

"We're going to wait until after the egg hunt," Brother Gregory said while all the workers gathered around him. "We won't scatter the wooden eggs until morning. I don't want them to get wet with dew," Brother Gregory explained. "If you're going to help in the hunt, be sure to be here an hour before the start. People are always early."

When they dispersed, Charlie went to assist the abbey's sacristan with laying out the vestments for the Easter vigil in the wee hours of the morning. Along with Abbot Ambrose's vestments, there were four other priests, as well as six servers to get ready. Luckily, the abbey's sacristy was large and had enough counter space to accommodate everything. They finished in time for Vespers.

"Are you joining us tonight?" Brother Zachary asked.

"Sure," Charlie said.

"You know, once the brothers are all in their places, you could join us in the choir stalls."

"Thanks, I just might do that," Charlie said, recalling how Rick and some of the other seminarians would wait on the side and then slip into the empty stalls during Mass.

Charlie quickly rushed back to his dorm and changed into his uniform. He grabbed his prayer book and made it to the abbey church just as the brothers were proceeding into their choir stalls. After they were all in place, he slipped into the end stall on the top tier beside Brother Zachary.

During the prayer, Charlie followed along but stole a glance at Dougary who was across the aisle, center stall, bottom tier. Seeing his former tormentor humble and meek but happy gave Charlie pause. When Vespers was concluded, Charlie waited for his tier to leave before he slipped out the way he came.

~§~

The alarm clock on Charlie's nightstand rang out at four-thirty in the morning. Charlie quickly silenced it. Easter Vigil started at six, but as sacristan, he needed to be in the sacristy at five. He had just enough time to shower and dress to be on time.

"What time is it?" Gus groaned.

"It's time to wake up," Charlie said as he passed Gus's cubicle.

"But I'm tired," Gus protested.

"We all are. You can take a nap after breakfast. Come on, get up." Charlie was already standing in front of his locker. His voice was no longer a whisper.

He did not wait to see if Gus was up. He grabbed his towel and toiletries and headed to the showers. The hot water felt good against his skin but began to make him sleepy. He turned the faucet to cold and forced himself to stay under the spraying ice water. He was awake now.

When he entered Saint Nicholas dorm, damp towel around his neck, he noticed Gus was sitting up in his bed. It was start, he thought.

Minutes later, dressed in his uniform, Charlie walked into the abbey's sacristy.

"Good morning," Brother Zachary greeted him.

"Happy Easter," Charlie responded.

"The Altar Boys serving at Mass should arrive shortly. Make sure they are dressed and then have them tend to their preparations. At five-twenty, the fathers will begin arriving and dressing. You need to be available if they need assistance. Abbot Ambrose will arrive about fifteen minutes before we begin. Stay out of his way. He has his own routine," Brother

Zachary explained. "Oh, I almost forgot. He wants his chalice on the altar. Do you mind putting it on the altar for me?"

"Sure," Charlie said and carefully picked up the chalice. He took it into the sanctuary and placed it on the altar. Looking up, he stopped and gazed out at the empty pews in the dark nave. In his years serving as an altar boy, he had seen this view countless times, but this morning, something was different. He stood for a moment longer taking in the scene, then turned to face the back altar and genuflected before returning to the sacristy.

After the Mass concluded and Charlie had finished his duties, he and Gus caught up with the other boys outside the refectory for brunch. Sister Faith opened the refectory doors and let them in.

"Good morning," she greeted them with a smile. "Happy Easter."

One by one, the boys returned her greeting as they passed in front of her, single file.

To Charlie's delight, the head table was covered in fake green Easter grass. Six large baskets filled with candy-coated chocolate robin eggs, jelly beans, decorated boiled eggs, and a large chocolate bunny were placed randomly on top of the grass. A ribbon with a nametag told the boys which basket was theirs. The others took a cursory look at them while they headed to the buffet table but Charlie took a longer look. He thought about the care and love that must have gone into making their gift baskets.

Charlie turned to Sister Faith. "Thank you very much," he said. "You are all so good to us."

"It's our pleasure," she said. She leaned a little closer and whispered. "I put something extra in the bottom of your basket, Master MacCready. Please, don't say anything to the others."

Charlie was at a loss for words. He felt his cheek blush. "Thank you," he said and joined the end of the buffet line.

After eating a breakfast of sausages, scrambled eggs, and strawberry and whipped cream crepes, Charlie was full. He sat back and watched the others paw through their Easter baskets. As expected, Gus's cheeks bulged and he had chocolate smeared around his mouth.

"You are going to be so sick," Charlie warned with a laugh.

"Nah, um nawt," Gus responded with his mouth full.

Charlie sipped his coffee and stared at his basket still sitting on the head table. He wondered what Sister Faith had given him, but remembered her words. He waited until it was time to go before he picked up his basket and took it to his cubicle.

After making sure Gus was not around, he reached into the green fake grass and felt the bottom. His fingers found what he was looking for, and he carefully pulled it out. It was a small gold-foil box. Carefully he opened it, not sure what to expect. To his surprise, it was a shiny medal of Mary. He turned it over and found an inscription. *Charlie, May you always have peace. Sr. Faith.*

He stared at the medal for a while, before noticing the time. He had to be down to help Brother Gregory on the Great Lawn. He slipped the new medal onto his chain and tucked it all beneath his shirt. He rushed out of the dorm and down the stairs.

Brother Gregory was already surrounded by a group of young children when Charlie crossed the driveway to the Great Lawn. Their parents stood nearby, visiting with each other while they kept an eye on their children.

"Sorry, I'm late," Charlie apologized.

"That's okay. We're still getting ready," he said. He excused himself from the children and walked across the Great Lawn to where he had hidden the bag of painted wooden eggs.

"Why don't we use real eggs?" Charlie asked.

"Oh, we started out using real eggs, but discovered if not all of them are found, they were when the brothers mowed the lawn. Let's just say, what resulted was not pretty. So, we now have the children search for these wooden eggs. They trade them in for the real thing. We've also painted the eggs with glow in the dark paint. So, tonight, we will come out and search the grounds for any that were missed."

"Smart," Charlie said, sounding amazed. "What do you want me to do?"

"Take that bag and walk around over there," he instructed, pointing first to another burlap bag and then to the area closest to the driveway on the west side of the Great Lawn. "Every so often, grab a handful of eggs and toss them around like you're sowing seeds. No need to be particular and hide each one. We want the kids to find them."

"Got it!" Charlie said. He took his burlap bag and did as he was instructed. While he walked in a zigzag pattern scattering the eggs, he noticed more and more families arriving. They parked by the gym and walked up the driveway to the portico. The children were excitedly pointing at Charlie while tugging on their parents' arms. Charlie smiled and waved back.

When he finished, Charlie brought the burlap bag to the tables set up beneath the portico. Sister Margaret Mary and Sister Faith were busy arranging the stacks of large cartons of decorated eggs that the postulants brought from the kitchen.

"Put the bag in the garbage can at the end of the table," Sister Faith said. Charlie started to toss the bag in when she stopped him. "No! No! Line the garbage can with it."

"Oh, sorry," Charlie said and put the bag inside the can, draping the top edge over the can's rim. Sister Faith handed him a large, heavy-duty rubber band to use to hold the bag in place. When he finished, he returned to Brother Gregory's side. "Now what?"

"We wait for the Easter Bunny, of course," he said in a loud voice so the children could hear him. They instantly quieted down and began looking around. Brother Gregory turned toward the gym. "There he is!" he announced. The children began to cheer.

Charlie turned to see what Brother Gregory was looking at and saw someone in a bunny costume, complete with big ears and a fluffy white tail, come hopping toward them. He carried a large Easter basket filled with chocolates, candies, and a stuffed toy bunny rabbit in one hand, swinging it back and forth. He skipped up to Brother Gregory and stopped with a final hop. The children cheered gleefully.

"Looks like we're almost ready," Brother Gregory said. "What's that?" He leaned closer to the Easter Bunny. "Oh, yes." He straightened back up and reached into the pocket of his habit. When he pulled his hand out, he held up three wooden eggs. "Before we begin, there is something you should know. If you find a red egg, it means you will get a special chocolate egg. If you find a silver egg, you get a chocolate bunny. But, if you find a golden egg, you will receive an Easter basket like this one." The Easter Bunny held up his basket. "There are fifteen golden eggs out there. So, are you ready?"

The children shouted, "Yes!"

"Then on your mark, get set, go!"

The children rushed onto the Great Lawn, screaming and giggling. Charlie stepped closer to Brother Gregory to avoid being trampled.

"Here," Brother Gregory said. "Take these and toss them but don't let the children see." He handed the three wooden eggs to Charlie who put them into the pocket of his blazer.

Charlie looked at the children all scurrying about picking up the wooden eggs. In the distance he noticed a little boy about four years old, he guessed, dressed in a tiny pair of jeans and a pastel green, pink, and yellow plaid shirt. Every time the boy started to reach for an egg, a larger older child grabbed it. The little guy did not seem to mind. He hurried off to find another, but the same thing happened. Slowly Charlie made his way closer.

"Hi there, how many have you found?" Charlie said, and squatted down beside the boy.

The little boy wiped his eyes. "Oh, nuffin," he answered, and turned his little plastic Easter Basket upside down.

"Oh, I'm sorry," Charlie said.

"It's okay," the boy said as though consoling Charlie. "I'll find you one."

Before Charlie could say another word. The little boy trotted off, searching the ground for a wooden egg. Charlie glanced over his shoulder. The children were beginning to line up to exchange their wooden eggs. Charlie turned back to find his little friend. He spotted him by a tree, still hunting for an egg but finding none. Charlie went to him.

"Steo nuffin," the little boy said when he saw Charlie. "I fink they're all gone."

The look on the boy's little cherub face broke Charlie's heart. The child was not upset and seemed to accept that there were no more eggs to be found. That's when he remembered the three eggs in his pocket.

"Would you like me to help you look?" Charlie asked.

The little guy's shoulder raised toward his ears. "I don't fink you'll find anyfin."

"Shall we try?"

"Ok, but don't count on it."

Charlie's heart broke a little more. He reached into his pocket and checked to make sure no other child was around. When the little guy was not looking, Charlie tossed the red egg on the ground not too far away. "Hey, what's that?" he asked pointing at the egg.

The boy ran to it and picked it up. Turning around he held it out to Charlie. "Here you go," he said.

"No, you keep it. It's yours," Charlie said. "Put it in your basket."

The boy dropped it in his basket.

"Look over there," Charlie said pointing away from them. The little guy went to see what Charlie pointed at. When he was not looking, Charlie dropped the other two eggs on the ground nearby. "Hey, what are these?" he called out.

The boy turned around and came running. Charlie did not need to point out the golden egg. The tyke spotted it and picked it up. With wide, excited eyes, he showed Charlie. "Found one." He dropped it into his basket and then spotted the silver egg.

With all three eggs found, Charlie said, "Let's go get in line and turn them in."

The two walked back to the abbey. The line was long but moving steadily. When they reached it, an older boy stepped out of line and approached.

"Hey, Seth, what did you find?" he asked.

"A golden egg," he said proudly and held it up.

"Let me see that," the older boy said, snatching the egg from Seth's little hand. "Thanks." The boy turned away.

"Hold it right there," Charlie said, straightening his back and puffing his chest out.

The boy froze and turned around, the gold egg in his basket.

"Give Seth back that egg, now."

The boy reached into his basket and took out an egg and handed it to Seth.

"No, the gold egg," Charlie said.

The boy looked into his basket and took out the gold egg. He threw it at Seth's feet. Seth started to bend over but Charlie stopped him.

"Pick that up and hand it nicely to him."

Belligerently, the older boy bent down and picked up the gold egg. "Here, Seth. I was only playing with you."

"Fank you."

Charlie waited with Seth until he had turned in his eggs and received his rewards. Seth's mother came to the table when she saw the huge basket and chocolate bunny her son was given. Charlie slipped away and found Brother Gregory.

"That was a nice thing you did," Brother Gregory said.

"What?"

"Making sure that older boy didn't get away with taking the egg from the little one."

"Oh, yeah. I was watching him. Every time Seth, the

little guy, would find an egg, some older kid would beat him to it.”

“They start young,” Brother Gregory said.

Charlie looked at him, a bit confused.

“Bullies,” he said.

Charlie nodded and saw Seth and his mother approaching.

“Hi,” she greeted Charlie and Brother Gregory. “Seth told me what you did, helping him find some eggs. I just wanted to thank you.”

“It was nothing,” Charlie said, smiling at Seth.

“He has something he wants you to have,” she continued.

Seth took the chocolate egg wrapped in decorative foil from his basket and held it up to Charlie. “Here,” he said with a twinkle in his brown eyes and a big grin.

Charlie started to decline but Brother Gregory grabbed his arm, catching his attention. Brother Gregory shook his head slightly. Charlie understood.

“Thank you, Seth.” He graciously accepted the boy’s gift. “My name is Charlie.”

“Welcome, Charlie.” He smiled proudly. Turning to his mother, he said, “I’m tired.”

“Okay, honey, we’ll go home,” she said to him. “Thank you, again.”

“Bye-bye,” Charlie said and watched them leave.

“Hey, Brother Gregory, how long do I have to wear this?” the Easter Bunny asked.

Charlie’s eyes widened. “Howard? Is that you?”

The Easter Bunny laughed.

“I can’t believe you didn’t tell me you were doing this,” Charlie said.

“Well, I couldn’t let you have all the fun.”

“Hey, hey, keep it down,” Brother Gregory said, waving at some departing families. “Wait until all the children are gone before you lose your head, Master Miller.”

"Yes, Brother," Howard answered.

"Excuse me," a woman holding a camera asked. "Would you mind me taking your picture with my children?"

Howard remained silent and just nodded. He then hopped away, following her to where three little kids stood beneath a tree. Charlie noticed the boy. It was the boy who tried to take Seth's gold egg. Seeing him sandwiched between his two sisters both dressed in matching dresses and Easter bonnets, and holding a gold egg Easter basket. Charlie felt pity for the bully. It was obvious to him the boy's mother favored the girls. The boy did not have new clothes like his sisters had. The Easter basket he held was well used and small.

"That's so wrong," Charlie said out loud.

"What's wrong?" Brother Gregory asked.

"Oh, nothing." Charlie sighed and walked away.

GRADUATION DAY

Excitement filled the air in Saint Nicholas dorm. Rick, Gus, and Howard gathered in Charlie's cubicle. Howard opened a bottle of sparkling cider he obtained from who knew where. Rick shared a plastic bag of cookies his mother had sent him. Gus was all too eager to help him eat them.

"I can't believe it's finally here," Howard said, pouring the cider into a plastic cup. "Just think, tomorrow we graduate."

"I know," Charlie answered. "It's a little scary, the thought that after tomorrow, we join the adult world."

"It's only for the summer," Rick spoke up. "Then we'll all be back here for college."

Charlie took a sip from his cup. He wanted to tell them his news, but he did not know how they would react, especially Howard. "What are you going to do this summer?" he asked Rick.

"I have a job lined up. I'm going to be painting houses with a guy from our parish. What about you guys?"

"Well, Charlie and I are going to take a trip to the coast. We may even head down to California. Who knows?" Howard said, mainly to annoy Rick.

"You're starting off being adults pretty lousy. Playing

194

all summer? Shouldn't you get a job?" Rick said.

"Been there, done that, last summer I worked my—"

"Howard," Charlie interrupted him before he could swear. "What are you going to do, Gus?"

"I'm going to be staying with a family in town and working for the lady at the stationery shop. Brother Simon made the arrangements."

"I remember her," Charlie said. "She was nice."

"Yeah, I'm looking forward to it," Gus said.

Howard looked at his watch, then gulped down the rest of his cider. He let out a loud belch to the chagrin of the others. "Well, I gotta run. My dad's picking me up. I'm spending the night with him and my cousins. We're having a before-graduation party."

"I still can't believe Father Mark is letting you go home the night before graduation," Charlie said.

"Yeah, well, I'm special, or haven't you noticed?" he said, sticking his thumbs in his armpits and playfully gloating.

"You're not that special," Rick said dismissively.

"Well, have fun. What time will you be back in the morning?" Charlie asked.

"Early," Howard answered. "Father Mark said eight. Gotta go."

"Bye," Gus called, but Howard was already on his way out of the dorm.

"Do you guys want to hear my speech?" Rick asked.

"No," Gus answered before Charlie could. "I've heard it a million times already."

"No, you haven't," Rick said, sounding offended. "What about you?" He turned toward Charlie.

"I'll pass. I still have some things I need to do. In fact, I should probably go see Father Cecil before Vespers. Don't leave a mess," he told them and hurried away. Listening to Rick's valedictorian speech was the last thing he was in the mood to do. Seeing Father Cecil was only an excuse to get away.

He headed down the stairs to the main floor,

remembering how frightened he had been when he arrived at Saint Michael's five years earlier. Now, the abbey felt like home, and his life with his grandparents a pleasant and treasured memory.

He reached the foyer and glanced at the main doors, recalling the many times he had sat on the front steps watching the driveway, willing his parents to come for him. They never did, and now he was preparing to begin a life on his own. He turned away and entered the abbey church.

The sight of the sanctuary with its huge crucifix suspended above the altar still left him in awe. He took a deep breath and smelled the scent of flowers mixed with incense. It gave him a sense of calm. The sound of footsteps broke the silence. Listening to the pace, Charlie knew instantly who it was: Brother Fiacre, the gardener.

Right on cue, Brother Fiacre entered the nave from a side door. He carried a large arrangement of flowers that was almost as tall as he was. He walked to the center aisle and to Charlie's surprise, genuflected without losing as much as a petal. He placed the arrangement in front of the altar and left through another side door.

Charlie slipped into the last pew and sat quietly with his thoughts.

~§~

The next morning, Charlie woke up in the overstuffed chair in his cubicle. He had fallen asleep again while writing in his journal. He stretched and picked up the fallen book. Adjusting the ribbon to the next page, he closed it and put it in the box on his nightstand. He retrieved a towel from his locker and headed for the showers.

"Good morning, Master MacCready," Brother Simon greeted Charlie as they met in the hallway outside the shower room.

"Hi, Brother Simon. Do you know if Howard is back?"

"I believe Father Mark told him to be here by eight," Brother Simon answered.

"Yeah, that's what he said. I was just hoping he'd be early."

"You do know we are talking about Master Miller, don't you?" Brother Simon teased.

"Good point. I best get ready," Charlie said and pushed the door open. Suddenly, an overwhelming feeling that something was not right struck him. He stopped, letting the door close in front of him, while the feeling faded away. Once it passed, he continued into the shower room.

Moments later, back in the dorm, Charlie dressed in his slacks and white shirt. He took out the black necktie from his locker and went back to the sinks and mirrors outside the shower room so he could tie it properly. Out of the corner of his eyes, he noticed Rick, who appeared to be struggling with his tie.

"Need some help?" he offered when he finished.

"I don't know what is wrong with me. I can't seem to get it this morning. You'd think after two years of wearing these stupid things I'd be able to tie it in my sleep."

"Here, I'll do it for you," Charlie said, swatting Rick's hands away and taking hold of the knotted necktie. He undid the knot and began to retie the purple and black striped tie.

"Have you heard anything from Howard, yet?" Rick asked.

"No, but Brother Simon said he should be back by eight, so he has an hour or so to go."

"Is it true you two are heading to the coast right after the ceremony today?"

"I don't know," Charlie answered.

Rick cocked his head. "Well, Howard seems to think so."

"Howard thinks a lot of things. And if it gets your goat, even better," Charlie said with a bit of a laugh. "There, all done." He stepped back to let Rick look in the mirror.

"Thanks. You're really a nice guy," Rick said. "Sorry

about giving you such a hard time."

"Forget it, I have," Charlie said. "We're friends for life, right?" Charlie held out his hand to Rick.

"You bet," Rick said and wrapped his arms around Charlie and gave him a hug. When he let go, he looked troubled.

"What's the matter?" Charlie asked.

Rick would not look at him. Instead, he looked up and down the hall and then at the floor. "I won't be joining you guys next year."

"What? But I thought you wanted to go on to be a priest?"

"Oh, I do," Rick said, looking at Charlie. "It's just my parents are moving to Santa Barbara and I've been accepted at Saint Anthony's Seminary. It's closer to them."

"Oh," Charlie said, sounding disappointed. "Have you told Gus?"

Rick's eyes instantly teared. He shook his head.

"Come on, Rick, you have to tell him."

"I can't. It will devastate him," Rick said.

"Even more if he finds out next fall when he returns and you're not here," Charlie said. "Tell him."

"I'll try," Rick said.

Charlie knew from that answer that Rick was not going to say a word. "Well, I need to see if my grandma is here. I'll catch up with you later."

"Okay," Rick said.

Charlie pushed through the fire door and headed down the stairs. When he reached the second floor, the feeling that something was off hit him again. He held onto the handrail and waited until it passed. Walking slower, still struggling to suppress his uneasy feeling, he reached Abbot Ambrose's office and knocked.

"*Ave.*"

Charlie opened the door.

"Well, son, come in," Abbot Ambrose greeted him with a big smile. He stood up and walked around to the end of his desk and held out his arms.

Charlie gave his great uncle a brief hug.

"You did it," Abbot Ambrose said proudly. "You've made it to graduation. Did you think when you first came here that this day would come?"

"No," Charlie answered and sat down in the chair to the side of the abbot's desk. "I can honestly say the thought never crossed my mind."

"Well, here you are."

"Yes," Charlie said. "Have you heard from Howard?"

Abbot Ambrose shook his head. "No, but then again, I wasn't expecting to. Is something the matter?"

"No, not really," Charlie answered. "It's just I've been having a strange feeling that something is wrong."

"Like what?"

"I don't know. Maybe it's just pre-graduation nerves," Charlie said and shrugged. "Is Grandma here?"

"Not yet. She phoned a half hour ago that she was just leaving. Bernice couldn't make it, so Chester is bringing her."

"Oh no," Charlie said.

"Don't worry," Abbot Ambrose said. "The brothers and I will keep a close eye on him. I promise you."

"Good."

"Have you told her about your decision?" Abbot Ambrose asked, looking over the top of his spectacles.

"No. I was going to once she arrived. You don't think she'll be upset, do you?"

"Upset? Why on earth would you think that?"

"I don't know. I just don't want her to be sad."

"Son, my sister, your grandmother, is a strong gal. She only wants what's best for you and for you to be happy. She's not going to be upset. On the contrary, she'll be proud of you."

Charlie smiled and felt his shoulders relax. "Thank you. I think I'll wait for her out front."

"Okay, but don't forget you need to change into your cap and gown before ten. We need to get a class picture of all of you out front before guests begin to arrive."

"I'll be ready, I promise," Charlie said and left the office.

~§~

The midmorning air felt fresh and cool against Charlie's cheeks. From the top of the abbey's front steps, he looked across the Great Lawn toward the gymnasium. In just a few short hours he and his classmates would walk into that building to receive their diplomas. It did not seem real.

A car pulled into the parking lot by the gym. Charlie could not make out who it was. He hoped it was not his grandmother and that his Uncle Chester would not make her walk to the abbey on the uneven ground of the Great Lawn. The couple disappeared from view. Charlie guessed they went into the gymnasium.

A car pulled beneath the portico and stopped at the foot of the steps. The driver stepped out of the car and helped his passengers, an elderly couple, to the sidewalk. Charlie walked down the steps.

"Good morning," he greeted them.

"Good morning, young man," the older gentleman said with a smile and nod.

"Would you like to come inside?" Charlie offered his hand.

"Yes," the gentleman said. "Are you one of the students here?"

"Yes. My name is Charlie MacCready. I'm graduating today."

"Congratulations. You must know our grandson, Rick Walters."

"Yes, I do," Charlie said. "In fact, he's one of my best friends and our class's valedictorian."

"He is now?" the woman said looking at the man beside her. "He didn't tell us that."

"Oh, maybe I wasn't supposed to tell anyone. He might have wanted to surprise you."

"Don't worry," the gentleman said. "We won't let on we know."

Charlie held the door for them and waited until they entered the foyer. "The abbey church is this way," he said and led them across the tiled floor to the double doors.

"We would have been here sooner but there was a horrible accident downtown. A car was struck by a train," the man said.

"Really?" Charlie said, an anxious feeling beginning to stir. "Was anyone hurt?"

"I don't know but it didn't look good. What a way to start the morning."

Charlie opened the door for the couple.

"Oh my, what a beautiful church," the woman said.

"You may sit wherever you wish," Charlie told them. "I'll let Rick know you're here."

When he returned to the foyer, a group of people entered. Charlie smiled at them. "Good morning."

"Hi," one of the men said. "Where's the church?"

"Right here," Charlie answered and opened the door. "Is there someone I should tell that you are here?"

"Sure," the man said and gave Charlie the name.

"I'll let him know."

Charlie returned to the foyer and dashed up the stairs to the fourth floor. He found Rick and their other classmates in Saint Peter dorm. He delivered the messages and rushed back to his cubicle. The navy blue gown hung on a hanger from the partition. His matching mortarboard with its white tassel lay on his desk.

"Hey Gus," Charlie called to the other side of the partition.

"Yeah?" came the reply.

"You about ready?"

"Suppose so," he answered, sounding distracted.

"Everything okay?" Charlie zipped up the front of his gown and grabbed his mortarboard.

"Yep," Gus answered.

Charlie stopped and looked at Gus. It was all he could do not to laugh. Gus had his gown on backwards and was struggling to zip it up. "That's not the way you wear that," Charlie said.

Gus looked confused. "It's not?"

"The zipper goes in front."

Gus's lips flattened and his eyebrows lowered. He pulled his arms inside and turned his gown around. Sticking his arms through the proper sleeves, he quickly zipped up the front.

"Who told you it went on that other way?" Charlie asked.

"Never mind," Gus said. "I'll get even."

When the two reached the sinks and mirror, they put their mortarboards on and adjusted the tassels so they hung on the left.

"Can you believe it?" Gus said.

"Nope. We should check to see if Howard is back before we go down for our class picture."

They slipped into Saint Thomas dorm and quickly went to Howard's cubicle. All of his belongings were packed into a cardboard box on his bed but there was no sign of their friend.

"Maybe he's already downstairs?" Gus said.

"I hope so."

When they reached the stairwell, they came face to face with Robin Muster. He gave Gus the once over and Charlie knew by the look on Robin's face who had misinformed Gus. "There you are," Robin said. "I've been looking for you everywhere."

"What?" Gus asked.

"Not you. Charlie," Robin said dismissively. "Father Mark wanted me to tell you your grandmother is here. She's downstairs in Abbot Ambrose's office."

"She is?" Charlie exclaimed. "Thanks, Robin. We'll

talk later. Come on, Gus." He rushed down the stairs, taking them two at a time, until he reached the first floor.

The slick soles of his dress shoes made him slip and slide a bit on the polished concrete floor. Slowing down, he glanced over his shoulder to be sure Gus was coming. Once he caught up, the two headed down the main hallway to the abbot's office. He knocked on the door.

"*Ave.*"

Charlie opened the door.

Abbot Ambrose stood up behind his desk. "Come in," he greeted.

Charlie entered and looked behind the door to see his grandmother sitting in one of the two chairs. The other chair was occupied by his uncle.

"Charlie, my boy," Ophelia said and stood to give him a proper hug.

"Grandma, I'm so glad you made it," Charlie said while holding her.

"Of course, I would. I wouldn't miss this for anything. My boy is graduating. I am so proud of you." She eased up her embrace and looked at him. "Charlie, you're trembling. What's the matter?"

"Nothing," he answered. "I'm just so happy you're here."

Ophelia looked at him sideways. "Are you sure?" she said.

"Yes, I am. Grandma, I want you to meet one of my best friends, Gustav Kugele." Charlie stepped back so Gus could shake her hand.

"Gustav, what a lovely name." She batted his hand away. "Come here," she said and gave him a hug instead.

"It's so nice to meet you," Gus said, his voice a little strained. When Ophelia let go of him, he retreated to a corner in front of the abbot's desk.

"Hello, Charlie," Chester said from his seat.

The smile faded from Charlie's lips as his jaw

tightened. "Hello," he answered without looking at the man.

"Congratulations on your big day," Chester said. "Maybe we could have a little chat?"

"I've got to go. Pictures and all."

"We won't keep you," Ophelia said.

"Maybe later," Chester called out as Charlie followed Gus back into the hall and closed the door.

"Your grandmother is so nice," Gus said.

"Thanks," Charlie said as they entered the foyer.

Father Vicar was standing at the foot of the front steps with the other members of the senior class around him. He looked up at Charlie and Gus and his eyes narrowed. "Where's Miller, MacCready?"

Charlie looked surprised. "I don't know. He's not here?"

"Would I be asking if he were?" Father Vicar said. "Well, we can't wait forever. Follow me." He turned around and started across the driveway to the Great Lawn. The class, all dressed in their caps and gowns, followed him in single file like a bunch of ducklings following their mother.

Father Vicar led them to a remote corner of the Great Lawn where a photographer was already set up and waiting. A section of the choir risers was set up in front of a cluster of green fir trees. Father Vicar positioned the boys to his taste.

"Shouldn't we wait for Howard?" Rick, standing in the center of the first row, asked.

"No," came Father Vicar's sharp answer. "Now smile, everyone."

Charlie found it difficult to smile, standing on the top row and knowing that his best friend would not be included. Still, under threat of pain and suffering, he managed a smile.

"That was wonderful," the photographer said after he snapped off the first shot. "Let me get a few more, just to make sure." In all, he snapped fifteen times. A couple were due to Gus's stomach growling which made the boys nearby laugh.

When they were finished, Father Vicar told them to line

up in alphabetical order, which they did. Then he had them count off, and the even numbers were told to step to their right to form a second line. Once everyone was in place to Father Vicar's satisfaction, he led them back to the abbey.

When they reached the foot of the front steps, Father Vicar stopped and turned around. "We're early. We will have you wait in the abbey's reception area until it's time. Absolutely no talking. And, remember your place in line."

With all of the chairs occupied, Charlie leaned against the wall to the left of the reception desk. He blindly watched the brother at the switchboard answer callers and redirect them to the appropriate phone number. Charlie's thoughts kept returning to Howard and with it, foreboding. He looked around the room at his fellow classmates. They seemed to be oblivious while they whispered and laughed quietly with each other. Charlie looked at the clock above the door.

At forty-five past the hour, Father Vicar returned, dressed in his vestments for Mass. The boys quickly took their places in line. Charlie pushed away from the wall and stood beside Gus.

Father Vicar looked at the boys. There was something different about his countenance. He seemed troubled and a bit shaken. He nodded at the boys and turned back to the door. Opening it, he led the boys into the foyer where Abbot Ambrose stood waiting with Father Mark on his right. In front of him were the two altar boys, each holding the golden candlesticks. Robin, the new sacristan, stood at attention holding the processional cross. When he saw Charlie, he winked.

Charlie leaned toward Gus. "This isn't right," he whispered. "Where's Howard?"

"Shhh!" Father Vicar hissed. "Now, walk slowly up the aisle. When you reach the front pew, genuflect and take your place. Do just as we practiced yesterday."

Two ushers from the junior class, opened the abbey church doors. The boys proceeded up the aisle, removing their mortarboards as they entered the vestibule of the church.

All through the Mass, Charlie found himself going through the motions, and not hearing a word. The feeling that something had happened to his best friend grew stronger. When the service was concluded, the boys led the procession out of the church. Brother Simon met them in the foyer and directed them to the refectory while the congregation made their way across the Great Lawn to the gymnasium where the graduation ceremony would take place.

"Brother Simon," Charlie approached him privately. "Where's Howard?"

"Don't worry about him," Brother Simon said, doing his best to remain stoic.

Charlie hesitated, then walked away. He stood with Rick and Gus away from the other boys.

"Well?" Rick whispered.

Charlie shook his head.

"They have to know something," Rick said, turning his head toward Brother Simon who stood like a sentry by the refectory doors.

The doors opened and Abbot Ambrose entered. He walked to the front of the head table and looked at the boys.

Father Mark and Father Vicar entered and stood with Brother Simon. They all had a somber expression.

"Please come forward and take a seat for a moment," Abbot Ambrose said and stretched out his arms, directing the boys to sit together in front of him.

Charlie, Gus, and Rick stepped forward and took a seat behind the rest of the boys.

"Boys—young men," Abbot Ambrose corrected himself. "Today is one of the happiest days of your young lives. One that you should be proud of and celebrate. You have completed what for some has amounted to a thirteen-year endeavor. That is no little feat. You are to be commended. After today, you will begin a new chapter in your lives. I pray that our Heavenly Father watch over you and bless you no matter what path in life you choose."

Rick's hand went up. Abbot Ambrose looked at him. "Yes, Mister Walters?"

"Is there any word about Howard?"

Abbot Ambrose took a deep breath and his head tilted slightly. "As some of you may have heard there was a horrible accident in town. A train struck a vehicle."

The boys gasped.

"It wasn't Howard's, was it?" Charlie asked.

"No, thankfully it was not. However, it has created a delay. So, Mister Miller will be joining us as soon as he can.

"Now, in a moment, we will proceed to the gymnasium, but before we do, let's say a prayer for those who were involved," Abbot Ambrose said.

The boys all bowed their heads. Some held the hand of the one next to him. Charlie, Rick, Gus huddled close. He closed his eyes and silently said his own prayer. He was still finishing when Brother Simon tapped him on the shoulder. Charlie said "Amen," and opened his eyes.

"It's time to go."

The cool spring air felt refreshing. Wearing his uniform beneath his graduation gown made Charlie a bit too warm. He pulled at his collar to vent some of the heat and allow the cool air in.

The procession made its way along the sidewalk around the great lawn. Charlie began to think about his grandmother waiting in the gym. Finally, someone from his family would be in the audience. The thought brought a smile to his lips and a feeling of pride. His only wish was that Howard would make it in time to share the moment with him.

When they reached the gymnasium, Father Vicar stopped them at the door. Abbot Ambrose, Father Mark, and Brother Simon went in ahead of them. Father Vicar led them inside and stopped them in the entry between the bleachers.

"Once the music begins, make your way up the aisle and stand in front of your chairs," he said. He turned to leave, but paused and looked at them again. "I am so proud of all of you." With that, he left and joined the rest of the faculty at the front of the gym on the main floor beneath the stage.

Once there, Father Vicar stepped behind the mic and said, "Welcome family and friends. I would like to present the graduating class of Saint Michael's Seminary High School."

The band began to play *Pomp and Circumstance* and the boys began to file up the center aisle.

It felt surreal to Charlie that Howard was not in line behind him. This was the reason Howard had come back to Saint Michael's, to graduate with his class, and now he was missing it. Charlie stopped in front of his seat, leaving an empty chair beside him in case Howard made it in time. When the music stopped, the applause began. Charlie looked at the faces of those gathered in front of him and finally found his grandmother. She was in the third row on the opposite side of the gym. Surprisingly, his Uncle Chester was not beside her.

Father Vicar stepped up to the microphone set up between the graduating seniors and the matching rows of the faculty. He raised his hands and silenced the applause. Once there was silence, he launched into his welcome speech. Charlie did not hear a word. His thoughts kept turning to Howard and what was keeping him. When he looked at the speaker again, he saw Father Mark talking to the audience. Then the choir began singing, but it was not *Bridge Over Troubled Waters*, the song the class had chosen. It was *Graduation Day* from the 1950s, the song Father Vicar tried to get the class to choose. They had argued that one line of the lyrics talked about a prom which did not make sense because they did not have a prom. They thought it was agreed they would go with Simon and Garfunkel's song, but that was not the song Charlie heard when the choir sang.

After the song, Father Mark turned to the faculty and held out his hand toward Abbot Ambrose. The audience applauded while Abbot Ambrose took his place in front of the microphone. Father Vicar stood beside him to the right. Father Mark stood to the abbot's left, behind a small table with a stack of thick blue folders on top.

"We've now come to the diploma ceremony," Abbot Ambrose announced to the audience. He glanced at the boys and motioned for them to stand. Charlie looked out over the heads of the audience to see if Howard was coming.

Father Mark handed Abbot Ambrose the first folder. He read the name inside and handed it to Father Vicar. The first senior stepped forward, took his diploma in his left hand, shook the principal's right hand. Turning around, he took a step closer to the audience and reaching up, moved his tassel from the left side of his mortarboard to the right. When he returned to his seat, Abbot Ambrose read the next name.

Charlie moved slowly along the row, all the while repeating to himself, *Left hand diploma, shake with right.*

"Charles Mathias MacCready," Abbot Ambrose said into the microphone.

Charlie walked across the floor to Father Vicar. "Diploma left, shake right," he murmured aloud to himself as he accepted his diploma. He stepped to the center aisle and moved his tassel before starting back to his seat.

"Howard Franklin Miller," Abbot Ambrose announced.

Charlie stopped and turned his head in time to see Howard accept his diploma. His cap was askew and his gown a bit wrinkled, but he had made it after all. Charlie waited at the end of their row for Howard to catch up before returning to their seats.

"I thought you weren't going to make it," Charlie whispered as they remained standing.

"I almost didn't," Howard whispered.

"What happened?"

"I had a close call, a bit too close. I'll tell you later."

"Is your diploma signed?" Charlie asked.

Howard looked panicked and quickly opened his folder. "Yes," he said with a sigh of relief.

"Mine, too." Charlie grinned.

Once Rick was back with his diploma, Abbot Ambrose congratulated the class. The gymnasium erupted in applause.

Despite Father Vicar's adamant warning for them to maintain the dignity of the event, the boys, almost as one, took their mortarboards and launched them joyfully into the air. Like a boomerang, they sailed back down and the boys caught them. They quickly put them back on. Charlie glanced at Father Vicar who was glaring angrily at them.

When the applause died down, the boys took their seats. Abbot Ambrose looked at them and turned back to the audience. "At this time, I wanted to say a few words. Life at Saint Michael's is not for everyone. The boys have had a taste of what it would be like living a life dedicated to and serving our God. For most, that is all they need to decide this isn't the life God has chosen for them, but, for the rare few, they have come to the decision to continue along this path." He glanced at the boys again and smiled. "I'm pleased to announce that one of our graduates has decided to join our monastery, Mister Charles MacCready."

"What?" Howard said, looking at Charlie in shock.

The gym erupted with applause. Rick leaned forward and looked down the aisle at Charlie with his mouth gaping in surprise. Gus rocked sideways and bumped shoulders with Charlie. He smiled and nodded, and mouthed, "All right!"

"I was going to tell you this morning when you got back," Charlie said to Howard.

"Damn," Howard said.

"Howard!" Charlie frowned and shook his head. He spotted his grandmother. She was beaming proudly. Behind her he noticed Sister Faith. She dabbed the corners of her eyes with a white handkerchief.

THE TRUTH UNVEILED

The noise in the gymnasium was deafening as the graduates and their guests mingled and talked in the back half of the basketball court. Charlie noticed Dougary and the other novices tending to the long refreshment table. Dougary smiled and nodded approvingly when he saw Charlie. With a plate of small sandwiches, potato salad, and a piece of chocolate cake, Charlie headed back to his grandmother.

"There you are," Howard said when he caught up to Charlie. "Is that for you?"

"No. It's for my grandma," Charlie answered. "So, what happened to you this morning?"

"I was headed back to the abbey, following another car, when we stopped at the railroad crossing in town. I heard a train coming but didn't see it. The car in front of me must not have seen it either. It started across the tracks. That's when I saw the train. I honked the horn to warn the other car but they didn't stop. The train crashed into the driver's door. There were sparks flying as the train pushed the car sideways along the tracks. I'm sure the driver is dead. There's no way anyone could survive that. The car was mangled." He shook his head as though trying to erase the image from his mind.

"Are you sure?" Charlie asked.

"We didn't stick around. After my dad and I told the police what we saw, we left. I couldn't drive. My dad had to take over."

"How awful. I'm so sorry," Charlie said. "I felt something was wrong all morning."

"I keep thinking, had I been a little earlier, driven a little faster, it could have been me in front of that car and my dad and I could be the ones who...."

"Don't think about that," Charlie said. "It wasn't you. You and your dad are safe and you're here."

"Yeah, I guess you're right."

"I am," Charlie said, with a grin. "I better get this to my grandma."

"I should find my dad," Howard said. "I'll see you again before I take off."

"Okay," Charlie said, then headed across the room to where his grandmother was waiting.

"Oh my," Ophelia exclaimed when she saw the treats. "I don't know if I can eat all of this."

"Eat what you can, Grandma," Charlie said, handing her the plate. He sat down beside her and looked at the crowd. "Are you upset that I didn't tell you before?" he asked.

"Oh honey, why would you ever think that?"

"I just didn't know how or what to say."

"It's all right, my dear," she said and patted his knee. "I could not be more proud of you, and I'm sure your parents would have been also."

Charlie looked at his grandmother. "Grandma, do you really think they are still alive?"

"I like to think they are," Ophelia answered. "Don't you?"

"To be honest, I'm not sure I do anymore, and worse, that I care. I mean, if they are alive, why haven't they come back for me? What is so horrible that they would have to stay away?"

"I wish I knew, dear."

"Grandma, what happened that night?"

"I don't know exactly. Your mother brought you to the house. She was upset and shaking. She handed you to me and told me to look after you, that she would be back as soon as she could. I tried to get her to come in, or at least tell me what was going on, but she wouldn't. She left, and that was the last I saw of her."

"So, that's it?"

"No. I called Chester to ask him to go over to your parents' house and check on them. He wasn't home. One of the boys answered, and said he went somewhere. So, I had your grandfather go see. He was gone for over an hour. When he came back, he had a worried look on his face. He said the house was a shambles inside, like someone thrashed it looking for something. The most worrisome thing, though, was that your grandfather found some bloody towels on the floor in the living room. I couldn't imagine why anyone would have done such a thing.

"The next morning, while going through the bag of clothes and toys your mother left, I found an envelope with the locket, key, and medal. There was a note with instructions. The same ones I gave to you when I gave you the key. That's when I knew why, but I did not know who.

"Charlie, I honestly don't know if they are alive or dead, but I have to hope, I have to believe my little girl is still out there, somewhere."

"I wish I still did, Grandma," Charlie said. "I mean, all I ever wanted was for them to come back and for us to be a family like the other boys have. Now, it's too late. I'm past needing them."

"Oh, honey, no matter how old you are, you will always need your parents. Trust me. I still miss my own."

"There you are," Chester interrupted as he walked up to them. "Hey, I thought we were going to have a little talk."

"Not now," Charlie said.

"Excuse me?" Chester said, and clenched his teeth.

"Go ahead, son," Ophelia said. "I'll be fine. Plus, I should eat something." She eyed the plate on her lap.

"I'll be right back," Charlie said. He kissed her cheek and stood up. "What?" he said to Chester.

"Not here. It's too noisy. Outside."

Charlie followed his uncle out the main doors, across the plaza to the Great Lawn. An uneasy feeling came over him when he realized how far Chester was taking him away from the eyes and ears of others.

Chester stopped and turned around to face his nephew. Charlie was no longer shorter than his uncle and was surprised when he realized they were the same height. Still, Chester had the advantage of girth and strength.

"I know you have the key and the box," Chester said, bluntly. "Since you will be joining the monastery, you can hand both of them over to me."

"I'm not giving you a thing," Charlie said, feeling his confidence replace his fear and nervousness. "There was a time when you frightened me, but not anymore. So, you can forget about it."

"You, insolent little brat," Chester snarled. "How dare you speak to me like that?" His anger rose like the red mercury in a thermometer until his face turned purple. He raised his hand to strike Charlie.

Charlie straightened his back and raised his chin. His jaw clinched and his eyes narrowed, defying his mother's brother to strike him. To Charlie's surprise, Chester huffed and puffed, then lowered his hand.

"You're joining the monastery. You have no need that money."

"That money belongs to my father," Charlie said.

"Your father is dead. I should know. I killed him."

Chester's words caught Charlie off guard. His shoulders slumped and Chester made his move.

"Now give me that key!" He grabbed Charlie around the throat and held fast.

Instantly, Charlie's hands clasped around Chester's arms and pulled against them. Chester's grip was too strong.

"Look here, you wretched little brat. You can either hand it over or I will take it off your dead body."

"You still won't have the box," Charlie said, gasping and choking.

Chester's grip eased, letting Charlie breathe again.

"Where's the box?" Chester demanded.

"It's someplace where you will never get it," Abbot Ambrose said.

Chester's eyes registered shock. He spun Charlie around and locked his neck in an arm hold. "Come any closer and he dies," Chester warned.

"Chester Allen Zenner, let my grandson go!" Ophelia demanded, standing beside the abbot.

"I can't, Ma," Chester said. "I need that money."

"Chester, what mess have you gotten yourself into this time?" Ophelia demanded.

"I owed some people a lot of money, Ma."

"Who did you owe money to?" Abbot Ambrose asked.

"I don't know. Just some people I met at the casino. After I lost all of my money, I told them about Patrick's stash and that I could get my hands on it, so they loaned me a lot of money, but I kept losing. They demanded I repay them. So, I waited until Faith and the kid weren't home and went to see Patrick. I thought he would feel sorry for me and help me out, but I was wrong. He just laughed at me and told me I was a waste of his time. So, I showed him."

"What did you do?" Ophelia gasped.

"I hit him and then hit him some more. The little maggot wouldn't even fight back. I kept asking him where the key was but he wouldn't tell me. He kept laughing. So, I grabbed a lamp and hit him over the head. He collapsed and wasn't breathing. I didn't intend to kill him.

"After that, I panicked. I searched the house and couldn't find that goddamned key anywhere. I heard a car pull into the driveway, so I slipped out the back. I had parked a block away.

"I went home and waited for the police to come for me, but when one day turned into a week, a month, a year, I figured I was safe. I vowed to stay away from the casinos and I did for a long time. But then I started up again. I lost the house. Susan left me. She won't come back unless I fix things. I need that money.

"It wasn't until five years ago, the day Charlie left to come here that I saw key. And it's mine," he snarled and tightened his arm around Charlie's neck.

"What about those men you owed?" Abbot Ambrose asked.

"When I told them I killed Patrick trying to get the money, they backed away and disappeared," Chester said.

Sister Faith, who had followed Ophelia and was standing behind her listening and watching what was unfolding. She saw the frightened expression on Charlie's face as he struggled to breathe. "Let him go!" she ordered.

Charlie felt his uncle flinch at the sound of Sister Faith's voice. But then he tightened his hold again and Charlie began to squirm.

"You heard the Sister. Let him go," Abbot Ambrose said sternly.

"Not until he gives me the key."

"Chester, take your hands off him this instant," Ophelia demanded.

Charlie twisted and pulled against Chester's grip as he gasped for air.

Before anyone knew what was happening, Father Mark descended upon Chester from behind. With his elbow, he landed a blow to Chester's back, knocking Chester off balance and causing him to release Charlie, who staggered forward. Incensed, Chester turned on the priest. He came at the monk with clenched fists.

Ophelia and Sister Faith caught Charlie and escorted

him away. Turning back, they watched the fight that ensued.

Chester swung at Father Mark, but his blow was blocked and met with a sharp punch to his gut. Winded but not giving up, Chester tried again and again, each time being met by a superior fighter, this time being struck in the jaw. Like an angry bear, Chester charged Father Mark and tackled him to the ground. Even in his habit, Father Mark managed to turn the tables on Chester and freed himself before Chester could land a punch. With both back on their feet, Chester made one last angry charge but was met with an uppercut to the chin. It sent him over backward and to the ground. Winded and gasping for air, Chester was done.

"Now, get up!" Father Mark's voice thundered.

Chester did not move.

Father Mark grabbed Chester's arm and pulled him to his feet. Chester kept his hands over his bleeding nose. Father Mark pulled a handkerchief from the pocket of his habit and handed it to Chester. "Here. Use this."

Chester took the cloth and held it to his nose.

"Mark, take my nephew to the visiting room next to my office and see that he doesn't leave."

"My pleasure," Father Mark said. "Come on, you." He jerked Chester's arm and the two started across the Great Lawn to the abbey.

Turning around, Abbot Ambrose noticed that some of the parents and other students had gathered to watch. He held up his hands and called to them. "It's all right. Go on back inside and enjoy the refreshments."

Howard, Gus, and Rick emerged from the crowd and came to Charlie's side.

"Are you okay?" Howard asked.

"Yes," Charlie said, loosening up his neck and blinking his eyes as the fog in his head dissipated.

"Was that your uncle?" Rick asked sounding both shocked and amazed.

"Yes, I'm afraid it was."

"Boys," Sister Faith said, still holding onto Charlie's arm. "We need to let Mister MacCready rest for a bit. You can all talk later."

"Okay," they answered.

Sister Faith and Ophelia steadied Charlie as they started for the abbey.

Abbot Ambrose pulled Brother Simon aside and whispered something to him.

"Yes, Father Abbot," he answered and headed back to the gymnasium.

Moments later, in the quiet calm of the visiting room next door to Father Mark's office, Charlie sat on the sofa beside his grandmother, holding her hand and trembling. He stared at the gas fireplace across the room between the two windows that overlooked the Great Lawn. He wiped the tears from his eyes.

A noise in the hallway caused Charlie to turn around and look at the closed door. The voices he heard were not familiar except for Chester's. He sounded different. Not angry, not as if he were still fighting, but like he had given up. Charlie turned back around once the hallway went silent.

It seemed like forever before the door behind Charlie opened and Abbot Ambrose entered, followed by Father Mark. Abbot Ambrose walked around the coffee table in the center of the room and sat down in one of the two wingback chairs that faced the sofa.

"Chester has been arrested," he informed his sister and Charlie.

"Good," Ophelia said.

"So, it's true then," Charlie said. "He killed my father?"

"Yes, son. I'm so sorry."

Charlie nodded his head. Tears filled his eyes, blurring his vision. He wiped them away before they could fall. "I had a feeling," he said. "What about my mom? Is she dead, too?"

"No," a voice from behind him said. "I'm right here."

Charlie looked over his shoulder but saw only Sister Faith standing by the door. She took off her veil and unpinned her shoulder length blond hair.

Abbot Ambrose nodded.

Charlie looked at Sister Faith again. "But you're a nun," he said.

"No," she answered.

"No. No. No," he repeated, shaking his head.

"Yes, Charlie, it's me. I am your mother," she said, coming into the room and kneeling down on the floor in front of him.

"You can't be," Charlie said, and began to tremble.

"But I am." She looked at Ophelia. "Mother, tell him."

Ophelia sat quietly in stunned silence.

Faith reached out her hand to touch Charlie's face but he pulled away. Visibly shaken, she stood up and took a step back.

Abbot Ambrose motioned toward the empty chair beside him. Faith sat down across from her son.

Charlie would not look at her. Instead, he stared at the buffet cabinet against the wall between Abbot Ambrose and Ophelia. He could not think. It was all too much. He jumped to his feet. "I have to go," he said.

"Son," Abbot Ambrose said, reaching across the coffee table.

"Charlie," Father Mark said, standing between Charlie and the door.

"Please," Charlie whimpered.

Father Mark looked at Abbot Ambrose, who nodded to him. He stepped aside.

Charlie ran into the hall. He looked to his right and left. He felt as if he was in a bad dream with no way out. He pushed the door to the foyer open and started for the main doors.

"Charlie?" a voice said.

Charlie stopped and turned his head. Howard and Brother Simon were standing by the abbey church doors. Charlie rushed to Howard, wrapped his arms around him and sobbed.

"It's okay," Howard whispered while he held onto Charlie and rubbed his back.

Gradually, Charlie regained his composure. He looked up and noticed Brother Simon was no longer there. He was alone with his friend.

"What's going on?" Howard asked.

"My dad—Uncle Chester—Sister Faith—" Charlie couldn't form a sentence. His words were a mere list of names.

"Come on, let's go see Abbot Ambrose and find out what is going on?"

"No. No," Charlie said.

"I'll stay with you," Howard assured him. "It will be okay."

"Okay." Charlie finally agreed.

The two returned to the visiting room. Abbot Ambrose stood up when they entered. Ophelia, seeing Howard, made room on the sofa for him. The two sat down with Charlie in the middle between his grandmother and friend.

"Son, I'm glad you came back," Abbot Ambrose said.

"Why?" Charlie snapped.

"Charlie," Howard said. "Give him a chance."

Charlie closed his eyes and took a breath. "I'm sorry," he said in a softer tone.

"Please, let me explain," Faith said.

Charlie still would not look at her. Instead, he averted his gaze and focused on the sideboard.

"Your father was receiving threatening letters and phone calls from someone demanding the money hidden in the metal box. He didn't know who or why. So, we planned on disappearing, all three of us. I needed to get some things from the store, so I left him to pack and took you with me. When I returned, I found the house ransacked and your father unconscious on the floor. I assumed whoever did it was looking for the key and the box. But we never had the box with us.

"Without knowing who was behind the letters and phone calls, I didn't know what to do or who I could trust. I called the only person who came to mind that I felt would be safe, Abbot Ambrose. I told him what was going on and what had happened and he rushed to the house with Brother Simon. Together, they put your father in the van and Brother Simon drove him to the abbey. Abbot Ambrose and I talked. I couldn't hide from whoever did this to your father with you with me. So, I took you to your grandparents where you would be safe. I gave your grandmother the key, medal, and watch. I told her not to tell anyone about it or give it to anyone, except you. Then I came to the abbey."

"We ended up taking your father to the hospital under the name of Brother Patrick. He held on for three days but died from internal injuries and head trauma," Abbot Ambrose said.

"I was frightened," Faith continued. "I couldn't hide in the monastery. So, Abbot Ambrose arranged for me to live with the sisters in the convent abbey."

Charlie looked at her.

"When you came here, I was thrilled but it wasn't safe for me to come out of hiding when there could still be someone looking for the key. Then I heard about Mr. Duggan and how he almost killed you by dropping you out of the attic. That's when I knew I had to see you. Abbot Ambrose arranged for me to work in the kitchen but in order to do that, I would have to pretend to be a nun. And you know the rest."

Charlie did not say a word as he tried to make sense of everything that she said. He looked at Abbot Ambrose. "You knew about this all along?"

"Yes, son," he answered.

"You let me believe they were both alive," he said. "Why? Why didn't you tell me the truth?"

"I couldn't. I wanted to, but I also didn't want to crush the hope you held onto so strongly."

"Charlie, I repeatedly begged him not to tell you," Faith said. "I saw how you'd grown into a wonderful, kind, and loving young man. You were moving forward with your life. I didn't want knowing the truth about your father and me to ruin that."

"So, if Uncle Chester didn't try to kill me, you would have continued to play a nun and never tell me the truth?"

"I—I—I don't know," Faith said, fidgeting and looking at Abbot Ambrose as if asking for help.

"Ophelia?" Abbot Ambrose said. "You've been quiet."

"I suppose I have," she said, holding onto Charlie's hand. "I'm in shock. Dietrich, how could you not tell me the truth years ago? I'm her mother."

"We didn't know who was responsible for writing those letters to Patrick and eventually for his death," Abbot Ambrose said. "The fewer people who knew, the safer we felt everyone would be. You had Charlie and were taking such good care of him. He was safe."

"Until Chester stepped in," Ophelia said. Her eyes moved away from her brother and a distant, far away look overtook her. "He killed.... What will become of him?" She turned back to Abbot Ambrose.

"It's up to the courts now, but my guess is he'll spend the rest of his life in prison."

Ophelia straightened her back and pursed her lips. "I suppose it has to be. He made his bed. But you," she said, looking at her daughter and her expression softened. "I always knew in my heart you were still alive."

"Yes, Mother," Faith said and smiled as tears dampened her cheeks.

"What happened to—" Ophelia glanced at Charlie. "Where is the grave?"

"In our cemetery," Abbot Ambrose said.

"I've been in the cemetery," Charlie said. "I didn't see a headstone with MacCready."

"No, son," Abbot Ambrose said. "We buried him with his birth name, Patrick O'Sullivan, to conceal the truth and let whoever did this think he was still alive."

Charlie didn't respond. He looked at his grandmother.

She looked grieved. She gently squeezed his hand.

"We'll figure this out," she said.

LIFE BEGINS

The scent of pine mixed with the lingering aroma of incense inside the abbey church on Christmas Eve. Charlie could not believe that his postulancy was finished and he was now a novice. Slowly he followed the procession down the center aisle and into the foyer. He and three other new novices formed a line that led to the open doors of the student wing. As the congregation emerged from inside, they paused to congratulate the new monks.

"I'm so proud of you," Sister Faith said, giving her son a gentle kiss on the cheek.

"Thank you, Sister," he answered, and smiled.

"I must confess, it is going to take some time getting used to calling you Brother Dominic."

"That's okay, Grandma still calls Abbot Ambrose Dietrich. So, you can still call me Charlie if you want."

"Will you ever call me Mom?"

"I don't know. It seems a little weird still since you're a *real* nun, now."

"I suppose. But I want you to know, I will love you forever."

"Me, too," he said as she moved on down the line.

"Hey," Howard said, giving Charlie a punch in the shoulder. He stepped back and looked Charlie over. "It's a good look for you."

"Thanks, buddy." Charlie said, rubbing his shoulder.

"Suppose this means I have to start calling you Brother now?"

"Not really. I'm still me no matter what my name is."

Howard glanced at Sister Faith as she started down the hall toward the refectory. "Hey, I still can't believe your mom's a nun and a hot one at that."

"Howard!" Charlie said disapprovingly. "That's my mother you're talking about."

"Gotcha," Howard laughed, and punched him again. "Guess I best keep moving. I'm holding up the line. See you in the refectory. I hope they have cake."

Charlie rubbed his shoulder and watched Howard briefly congratulate the other brothers before disappearing down the hallway. He looked back at the line.

"Grandma," he said and gave Ophelia a hug.

"I'm so proud of you, Charlie," she said, pulling him down so she could kiss his cheek. "I want to thank you again for moving me to The Towers so I can be closer to you and your mother. You didn't have to do that."

"I think that's what my dad would have wanted me to do with that money."

"No, he would have wanted you to use it for yourself."

"I did. Having you close by is for myself." Charlie said.

"You are such a good boy," Ophelia said, kissing Charlie's cheek again and grinning at him.

Once the line had passed, Charlie and the other novices went to join the reception in the high school's refectory.

The refectory was decorated for Christmas. A tall pine tree stood in the corner between the head table and the windows sparkling and glittering with colored lights and bulbs. The scent of baking gingerbread in the kitchen next door made its way into the room. It stirred up memories of Christmas' past. Charlie felt anticipation for the holiday growing in his chest. He spotted Howard, Rick, and Gus standing together in the back corner beneath the frosted windows. He grabbed a cup of punch and went to join them.

"Hey guys," Charlie greeted them. "Merry Christmas."

"Merry Christmas," they all responded, though Gus was busy eating a large piece of cake.

"So, what's happening with your uncle?" Rick asked bluntly and catching Charlie off guard.

Charlie looked at each of his friends faces and took a deep breath. "Last month, he pled guilty and was sentenced to life in prison, just like Abbot Ambrose suspected."

"That was fast," Rick said.

"When you're guilty, you're guilty," Howard said. "Let's talk about something else. Rick has some news, don't ya, buddy?" He playfully slugged Rick on the shoulder. Rick recoiled and rubbed the spot.

"What was that for?" he groaned.

"Just a little love tap, ol' friend," Howard answered and laughed, though he glared at Rick, too.

"Well, don't do it again."

"So, what's your news?" Charlie interrupted.

"I've decided to transfer back to Saint Michael's starting next term. I miss you guys and all of our adventures."

"Weelwee?" Gus said, his mouth full of cake.

"Yes," Rick said. "You're gonna choke." He handed his friend his glass of punch.

"That's great!" Charlie said.

"It's gonna be like old times," Howard said. "The four of us together again."

Gus gulped down his drink. "What mystery do we solve next?"

Charlie looked at each of his friends in turn and laughed. "Let's just see what comes along."

* * * * *

ABOUT THE AUTHOR

Author James M. McCracken left home at age thirteen and was enrolled in a seminary boarding school operated by Benedictine monks, residing there for the next five years. That is where his love for writing stories began.

The years spent in the seminary are the inspiration behind the Charlie MacCready series, though the events in the stories are all fictious as are the characters.

Mr. McCracken is a longtime member of the writers' group, Becoming Fiction, and is the president of the Northwest Independent Writers Association. He currently resides in Central Oregon.